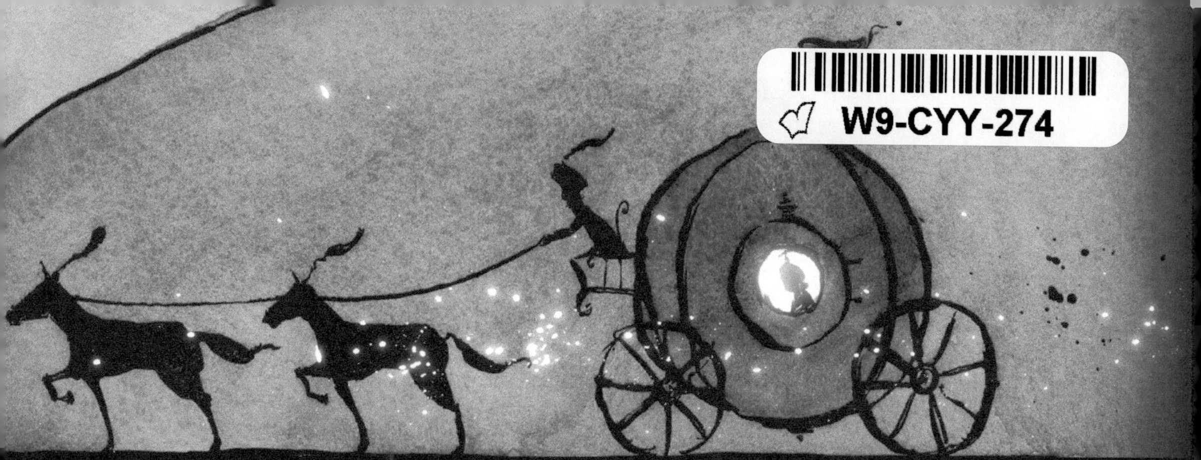

CINDERELLA

The Graphic Novel

retold by Beth Bracken illustrated by Jeffrey Stewart Timmins

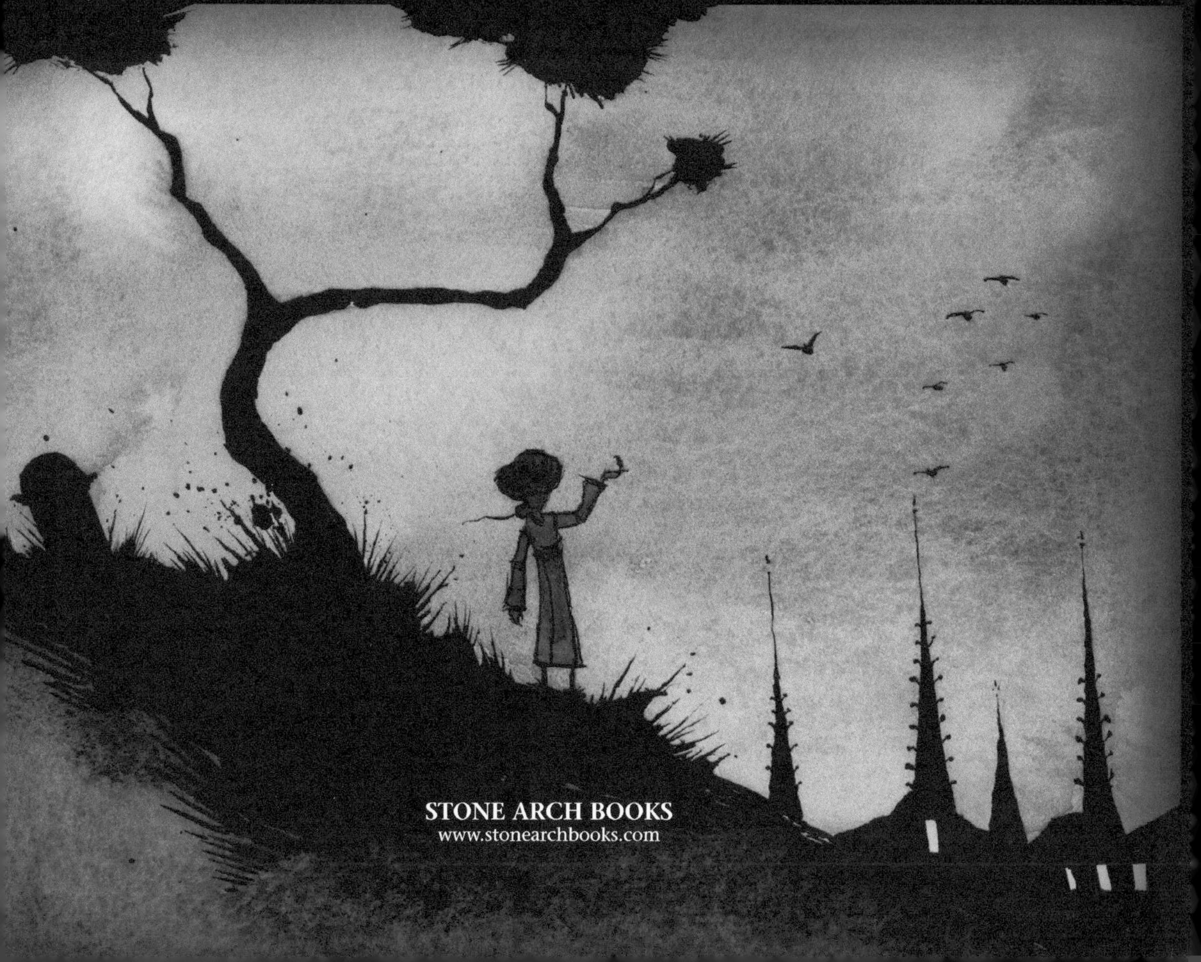

STONE ARCH BOOKS
www.stonearchbooks.com

Graphic Spin is published by Stone Arch Books,
A Capstone Imprint
1710 Roe Crest Drive
North Mankato, Minnesota 56003
www.capstonepub.com

Library of Congress Cataloging-in-Publication Data
Bracken, Beth.
Cinderella: The Graphic Novel / retold by Beth Bracken; illustrated by Jeffrey Stewart Timmins.
p. cm. — (Graphic Spin)
ISBN 978-1-4342-0764-7 (library binding)
ISBN 978-1-4342-0860-6 (pbk.)
1. Graphic novels. [1. Graphic novels.] I. Timmins, Jeffrey Stewart, ill. II. Cinderella. English.
III. Title.
PZ7.7.B73Cin 2009
[Fic]—dc22 2008006720

Summary: Cinderella's wicked stepmother won't let her go to the ball. But with a little help from a Fairy Godmother, she'll be getting there in style. There's just one catch. At midnight, her magical gown will turn back into dirty old rags.

Art Director: Heather Kindseth
Graphic Designer: Kay Fraser

Librarian Reviewer
Julie Potvin Kirchner
Educator, Wayzata Public Schools
BA in Elementary Education, The College of Saint Catherine, Saint Paul, MN
MA in Education, The College of Saint Catherine, Saint Paul, MN
MLS, Texas Woman's University

Reading Consultant
Elizabeth Stedem
Educator/Consultant, Colorado Springs, CO
MA in Elementary Education, University of Denver, CO

Printed in the United States 4512

CINDERELLA

The Graphic Novel

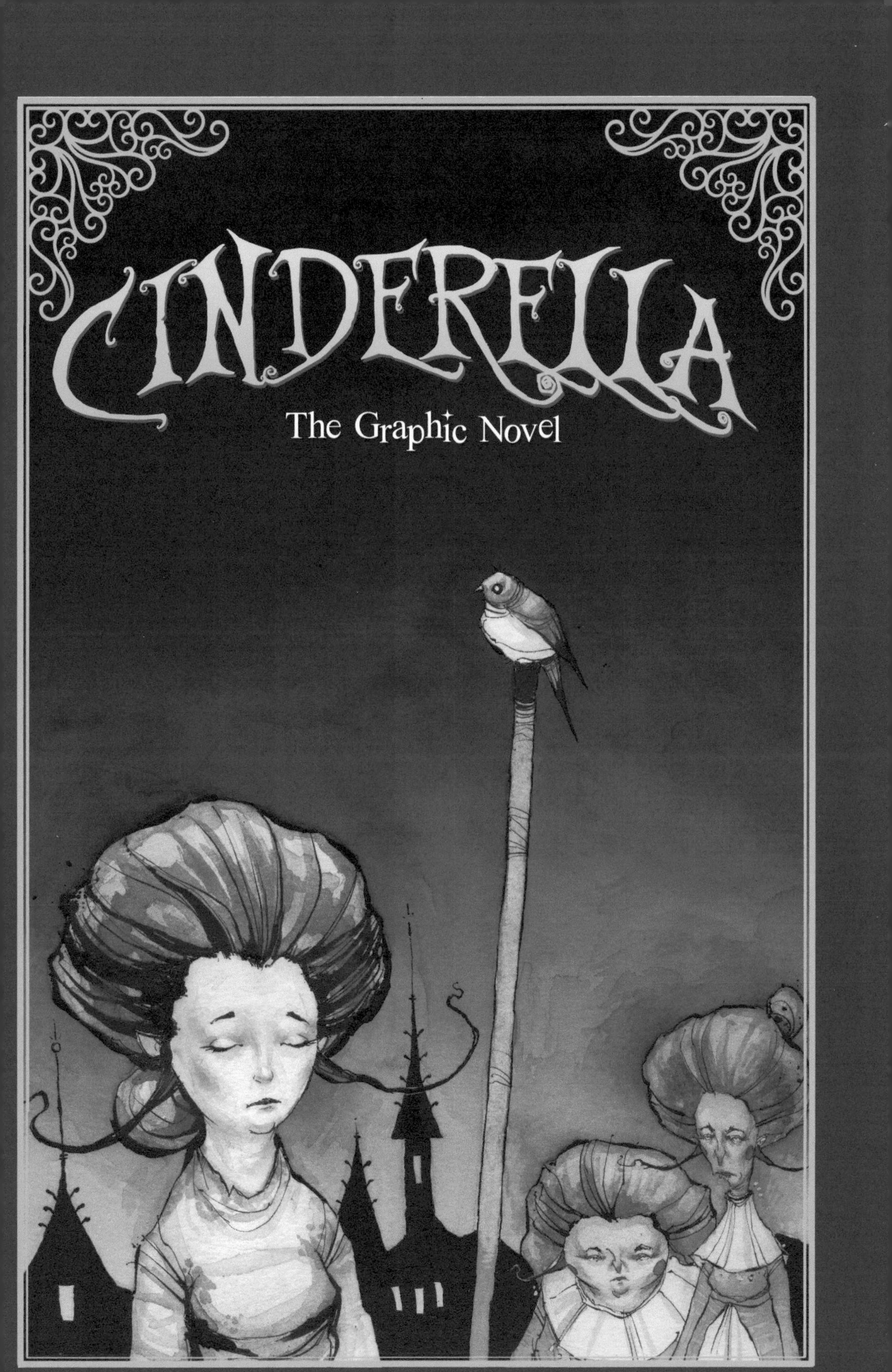

CAST OF CHARACTERS

THE EVIL
STEPMOTHER

THE EVIL
STEPSISTERS

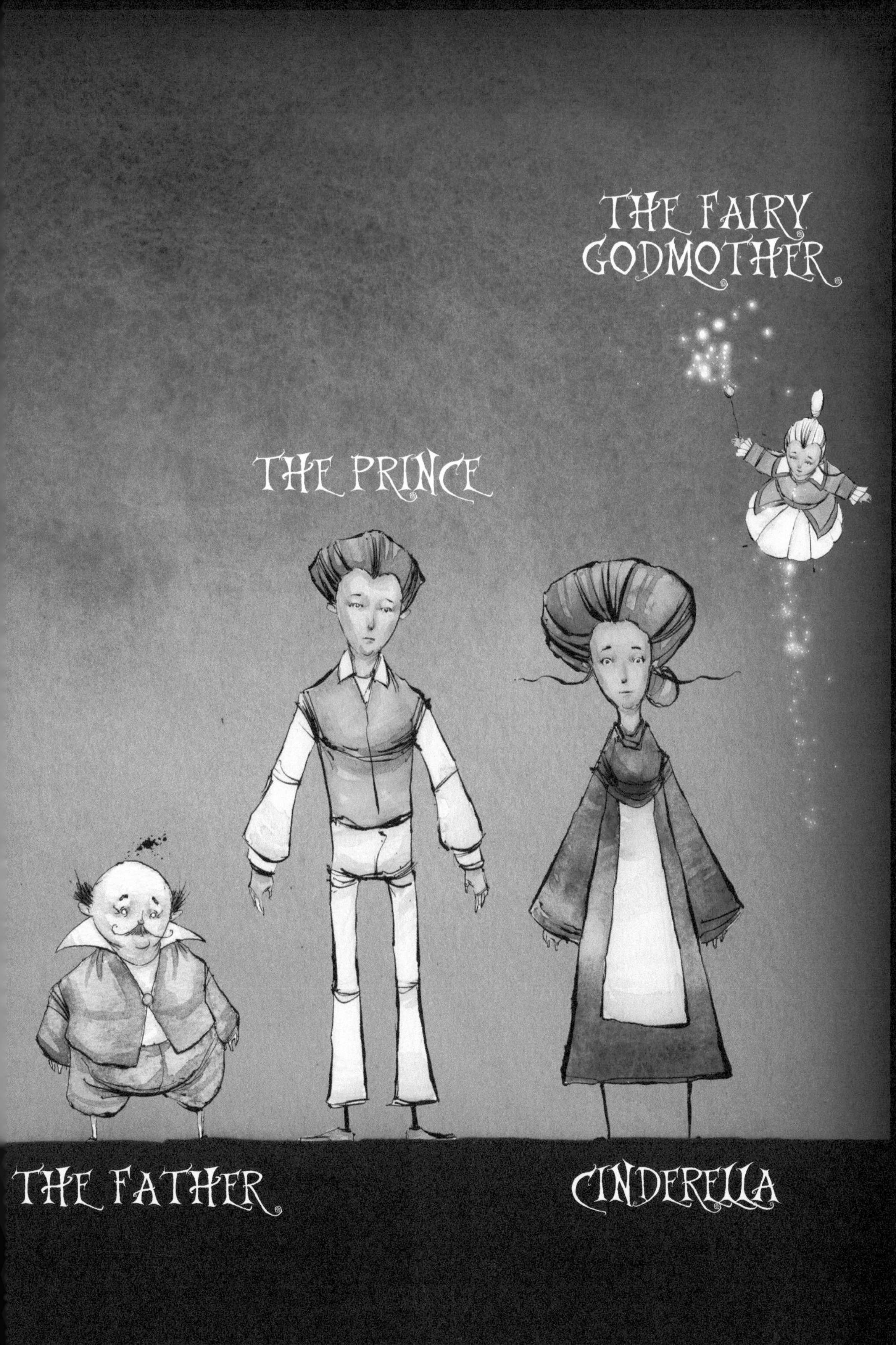
THE FAIRY GODMOTHER
THE PRINCE
THE FATHER
CINDERELLA

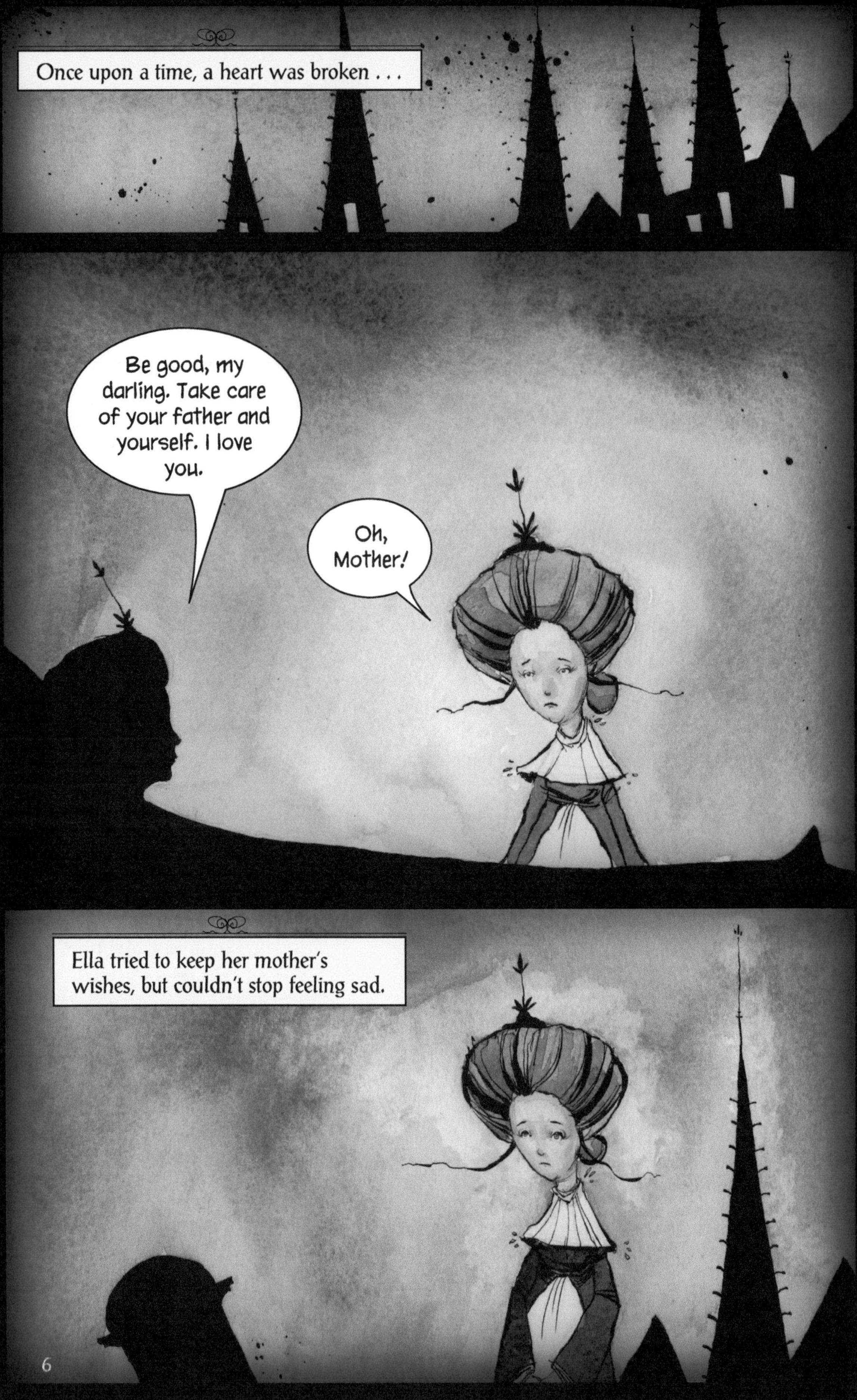
Once upon a time, a heart was broken . . .
Be good, my darling. Take care of your father and yourself. I love you.
Oh, Mother!
Ella tried to keep her mother's wishes, but couldn't stop feeling sad.

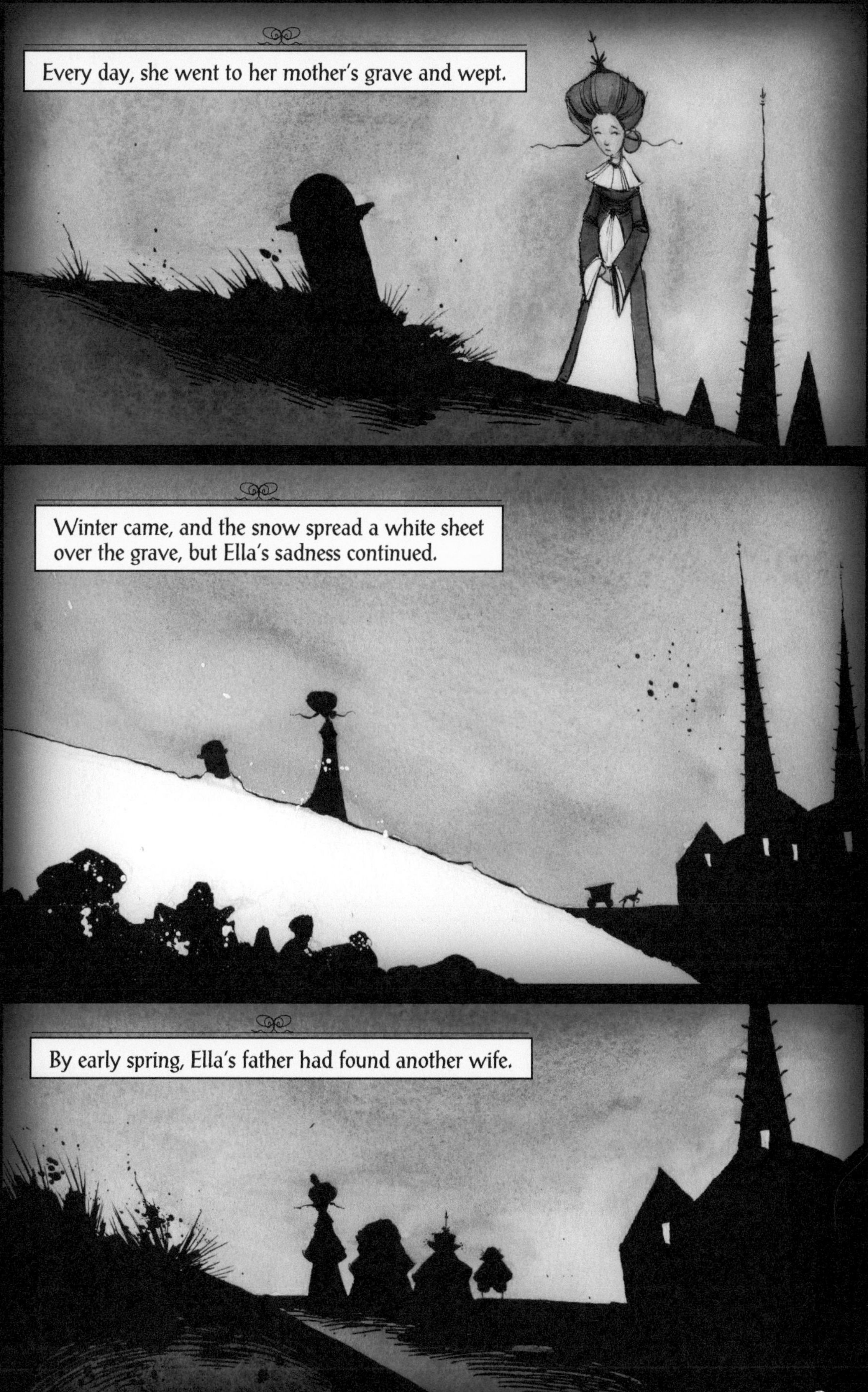
Every day, she went to her mother's grave and wept.
Winter came, and the snow spread a white sheet over the grave, but Ella's sadness continued.
By early spring, Ella's father had found another wife.

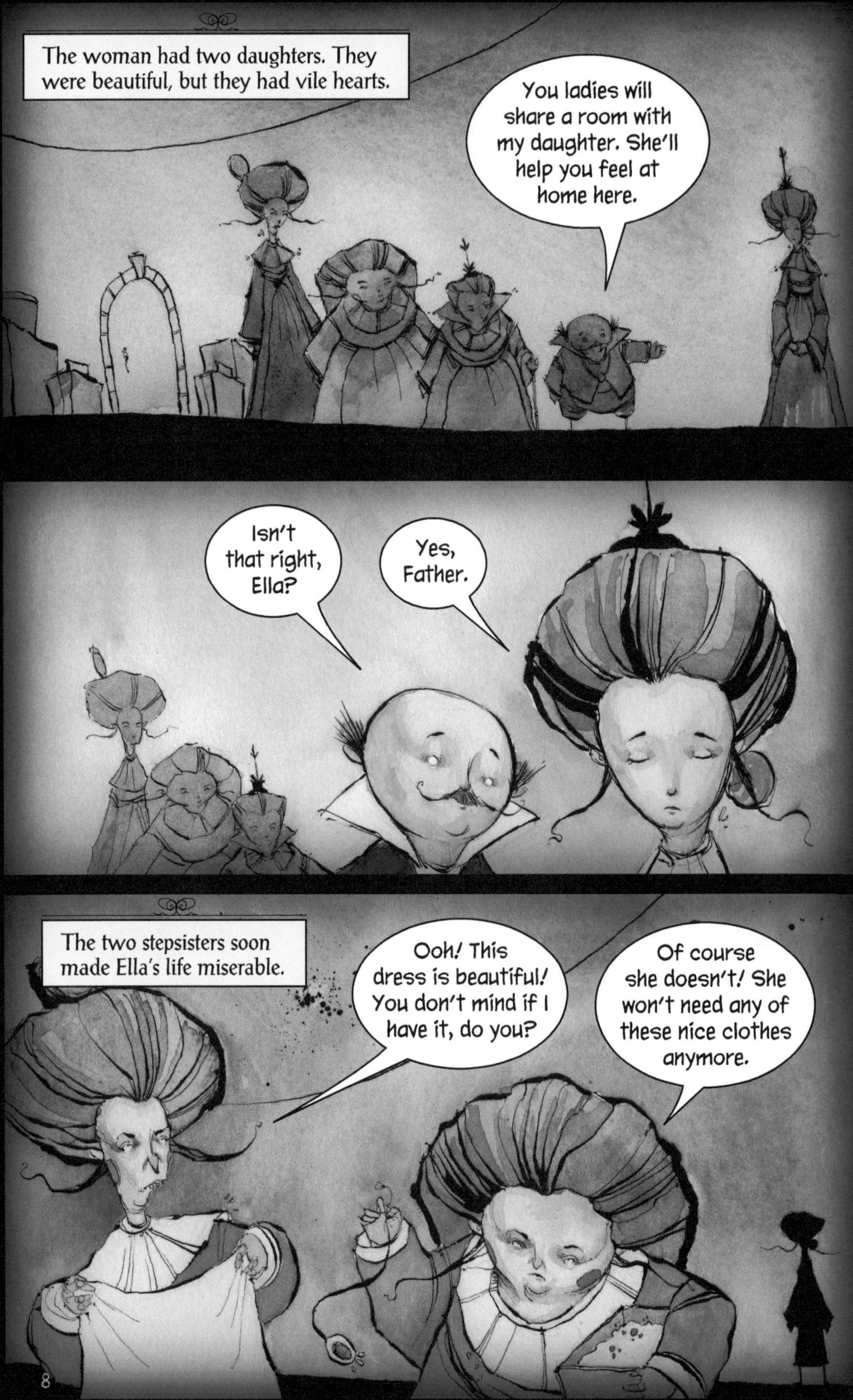
The woman had two daughters. They were beautiful, but they had vile hearts.
You ladies will share a room with my daughter. She'll help you feel at home here.
Isn't that right, Ella?
Yes, Father.
The two stepsisters soon made Ella's life miserable.
Ooh! This dress is beautiful! You don't mind if I have it, do you?
Of course she doesn't! She won't need any of these nice clothes anymore.

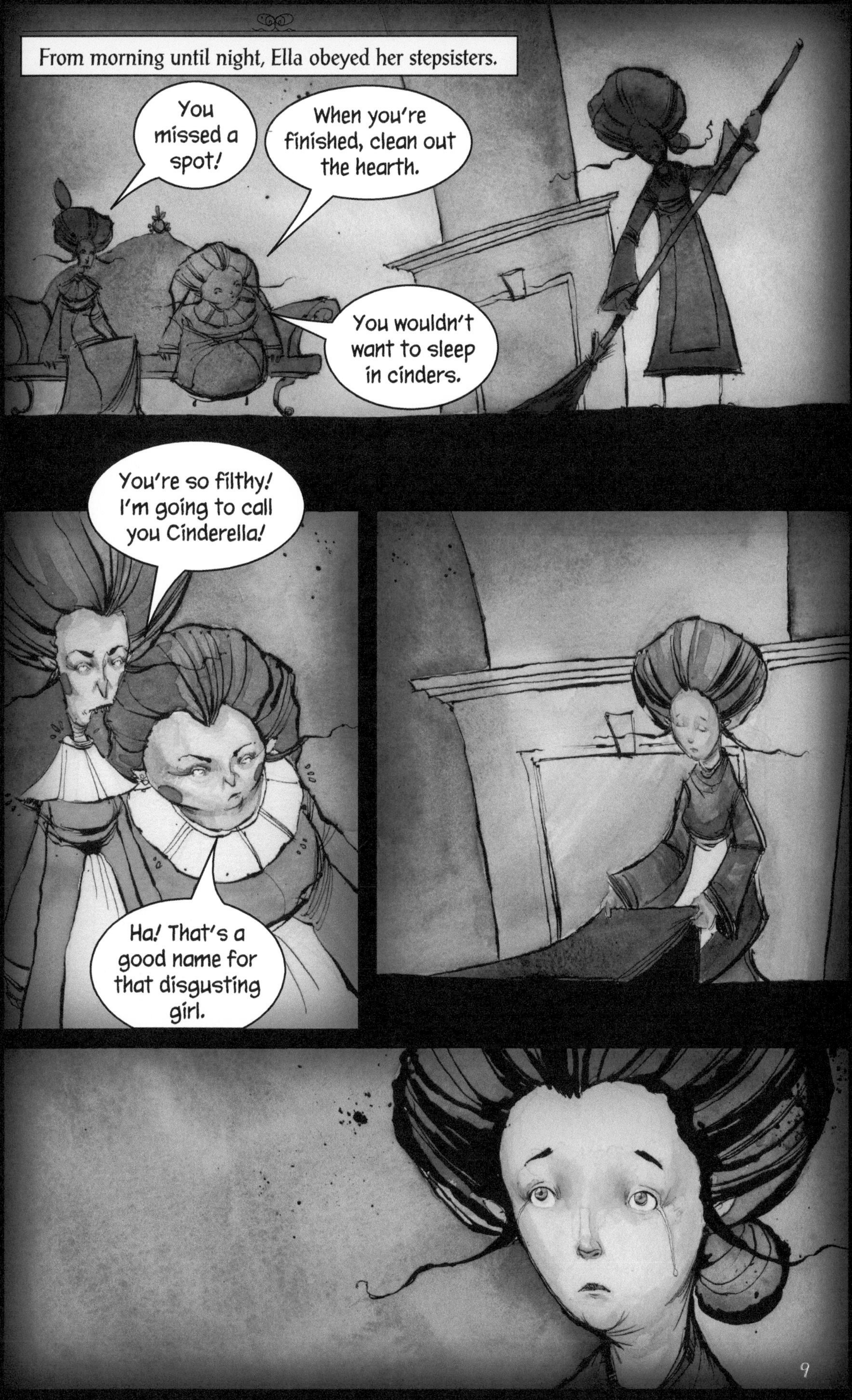
From morning until night, Ella obeyed her stepsisters.
You missed a spot!
When you're finished, clean out the hearth.
You wouldn't want to sleep in cinders.
You're so filthy! I'm going to call you Cinderella!
Ha! That's a good name for that disgusting girl.

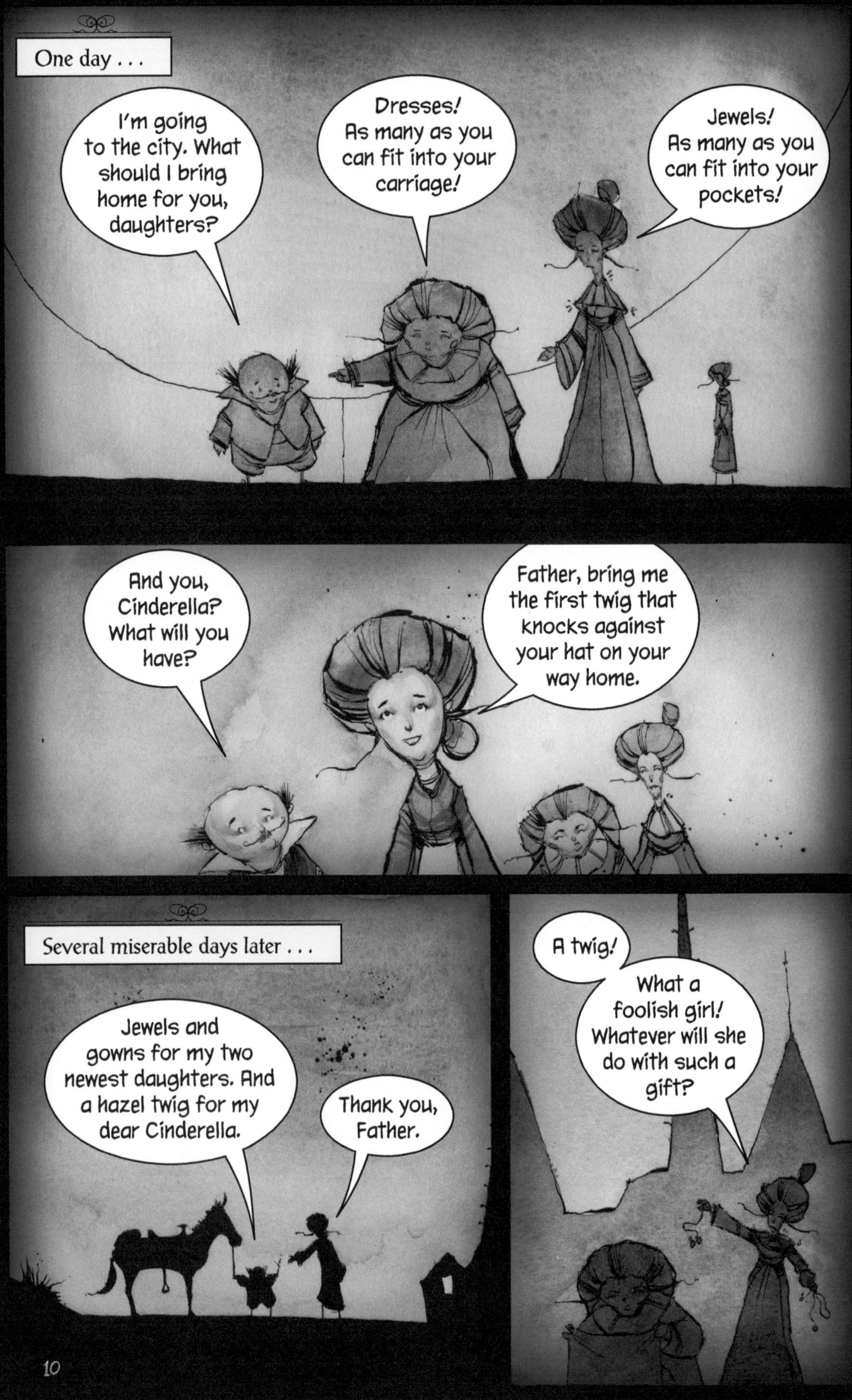
One day . . .
I'm going to the city. What should I bring home for you, daughters?
Dresses! As many as you can fit into your carriage!
Jewels! As many as you can fit into your pockets!
And you, Cinderella? What will you have?
Father, bring me the first twig that knocks against your hat on your way home.
Several miserable days later . . .
Jewels and gowns for my two newest daughters. And a hazel twig for my dear Cinderella.
Thank you, Father.
A twig!
What a foolish girl! Whatever will she do with such a gift?

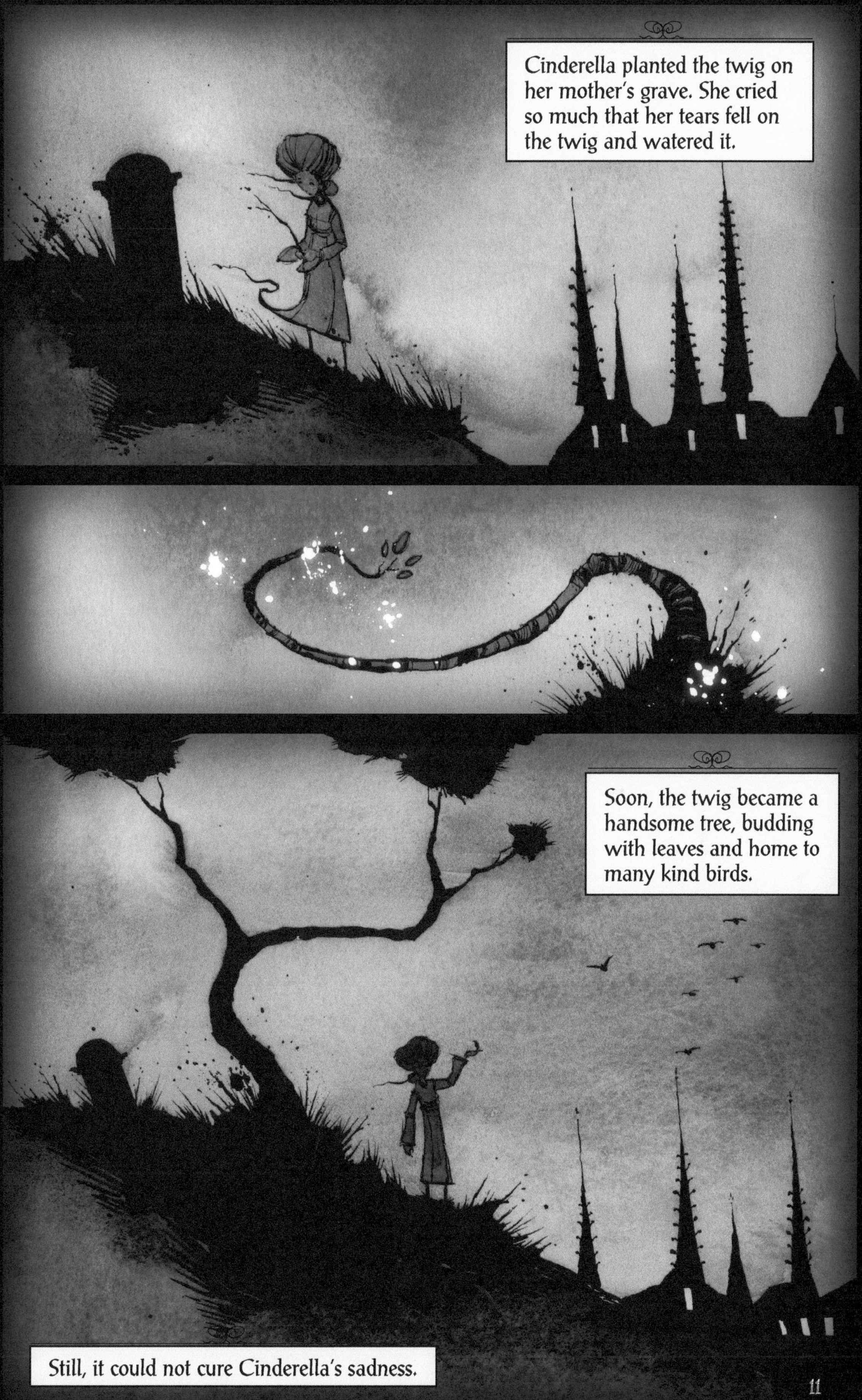
Cinderella planted the twig on her mother's grave. She cried so much that her tears fell on the twig and watered it.
Soon, the twig became a handsome tree, budding with leaves and home to many kind birds.
Still, it could not cure Cinderella's sadness.

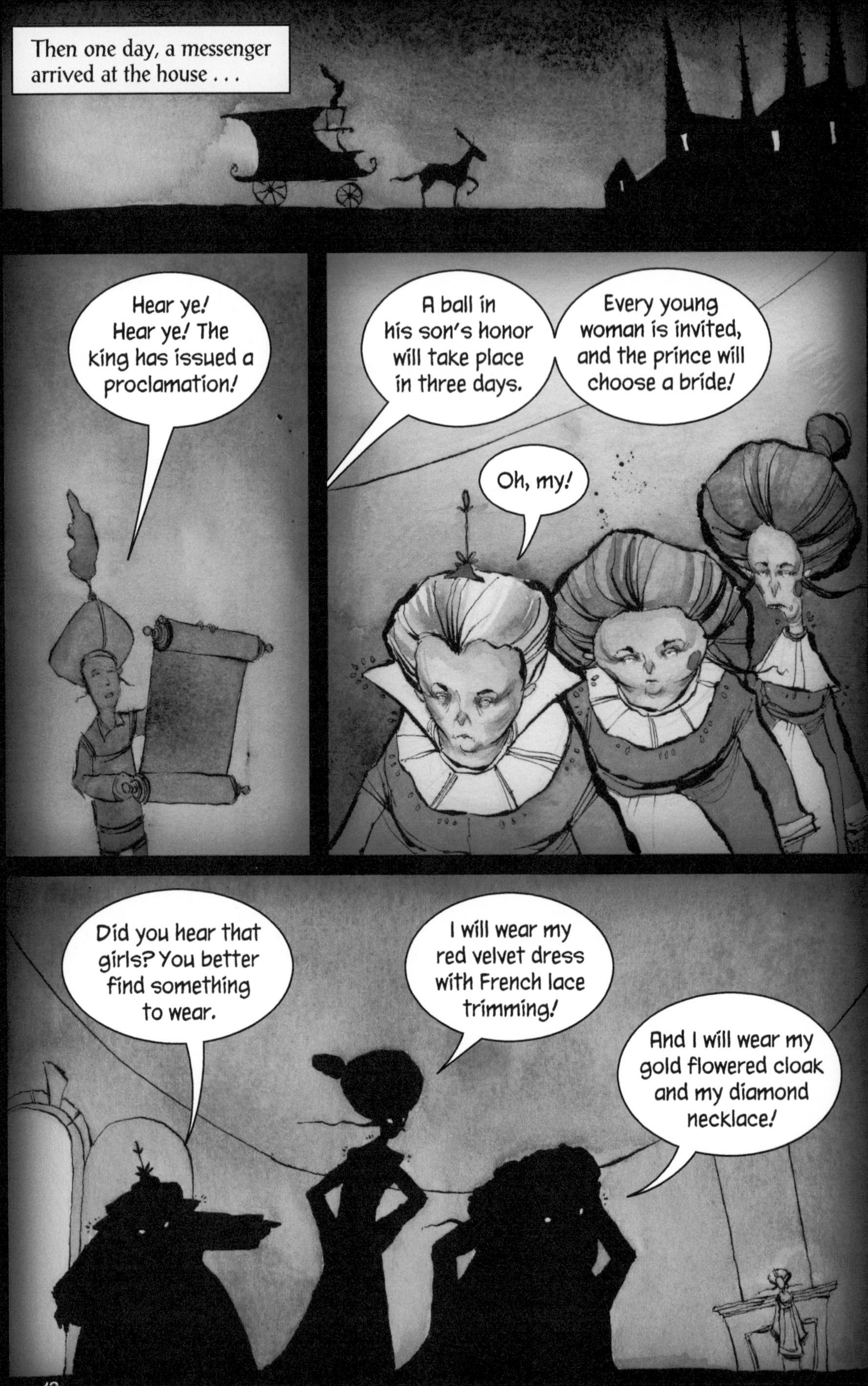
Then one day, a messenger arrived at the house . . .
Hear ye! Hear ye! The king has issued a proclamation!
A ball in his son's honor will take place in three days.
Every young woman is invited, and the prince will choose a bride!
Oh, my!
Did you hear that girls? You better find something to wear.
I will wear my red velvet dress with French lace trimming!
And I will wear my gold flowered cloak and my diamond necklace!

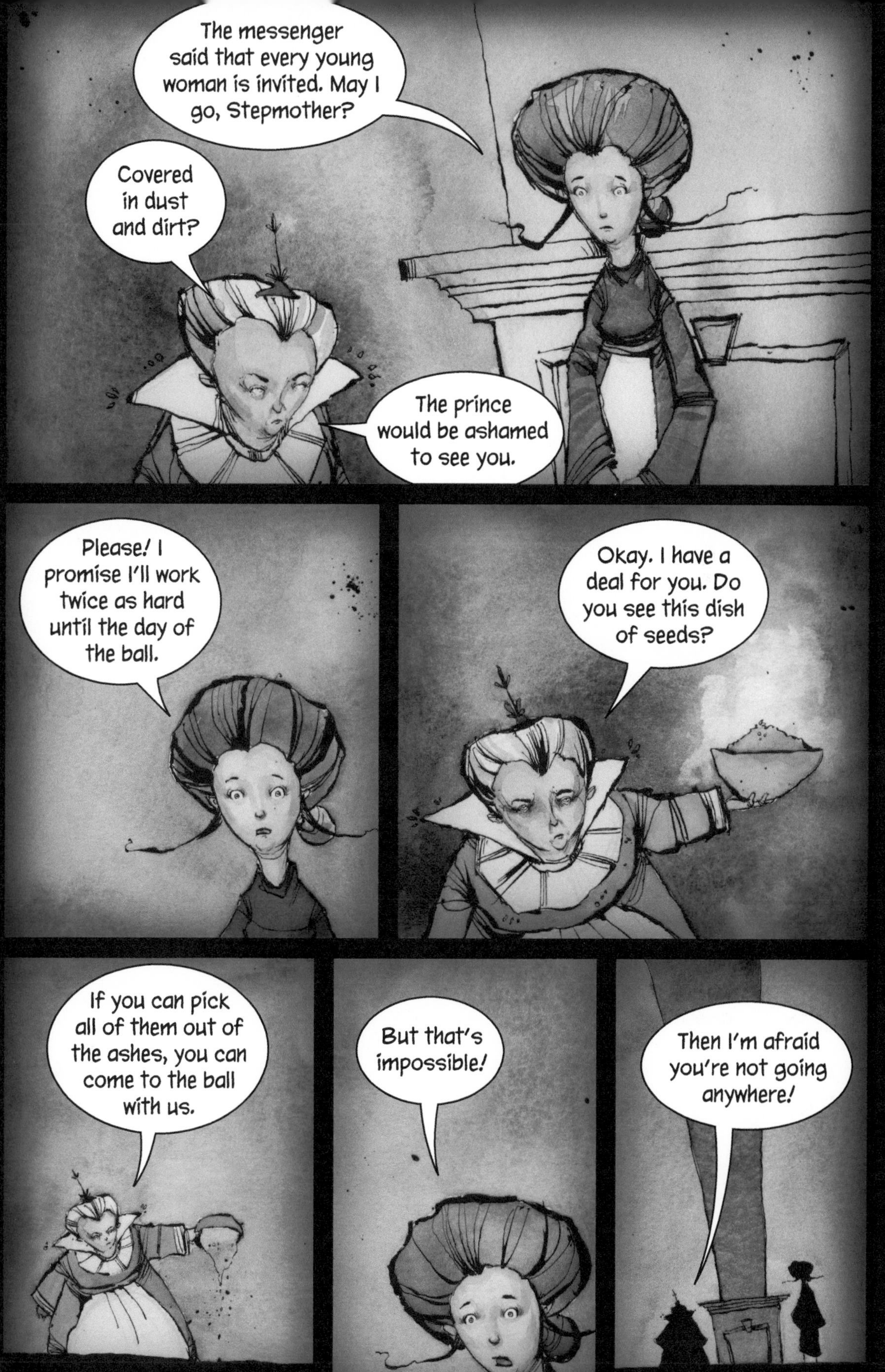
The messenger said that every young woman is invited. May I go, Stepmother?
Covered in dust and dirt?
The prince would be ashamed to see you.
Please! I promise I'll work twice as hard until the day of the ball.
Okay. I have a deal for you. Do you see this dish of seeds?
If you can pick all of them out of the ashes, you can come to the ball with us.
But that's impossible!
Then I'm afraid you're not going anywhere!

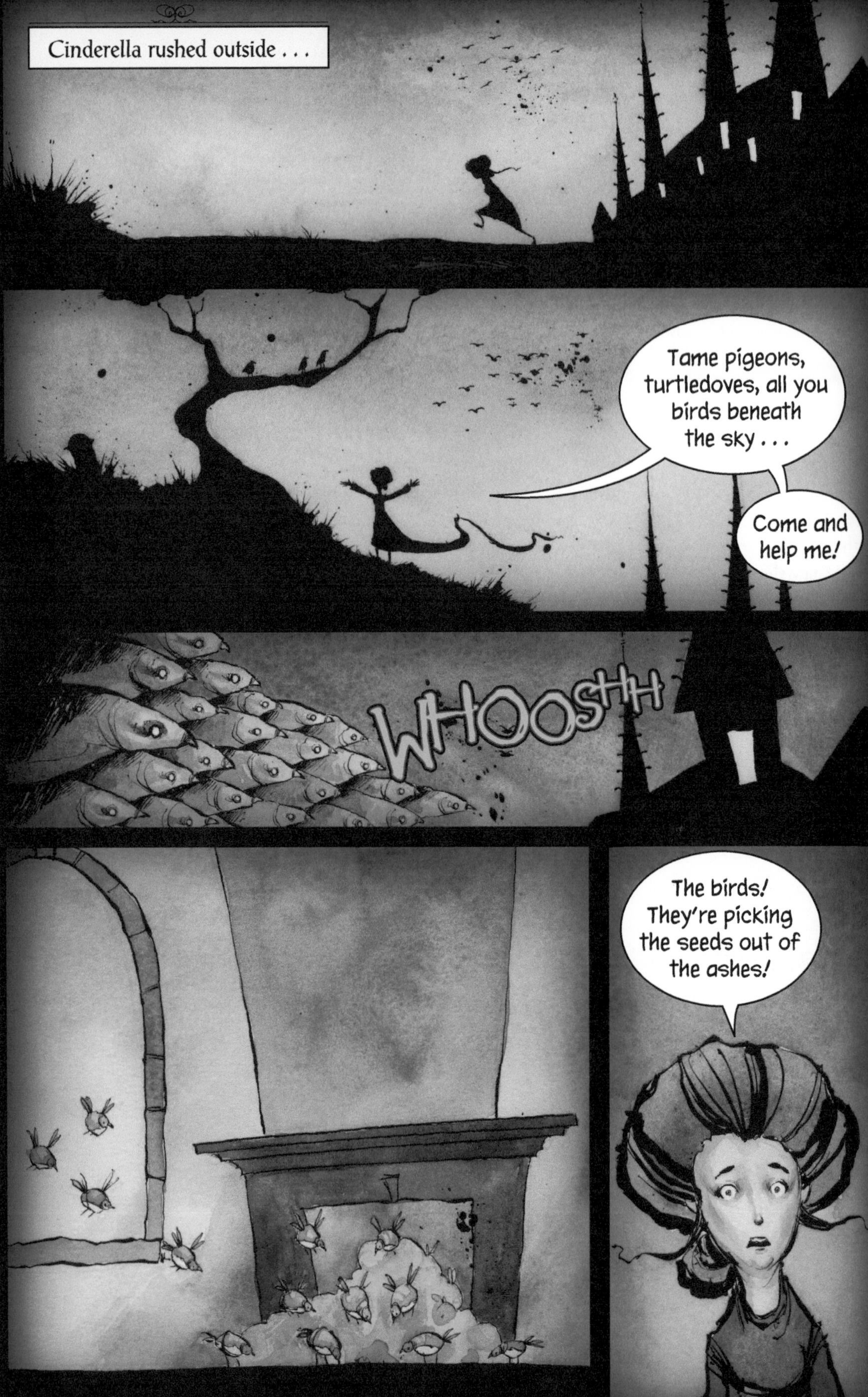

Cinderella rushed outside . . .
Tame pigeons, turtledoves, all you birds beneath the sky . . .
Come and help me!
WHOOSHH
The birds! They're picking the seeds out of the ashes!

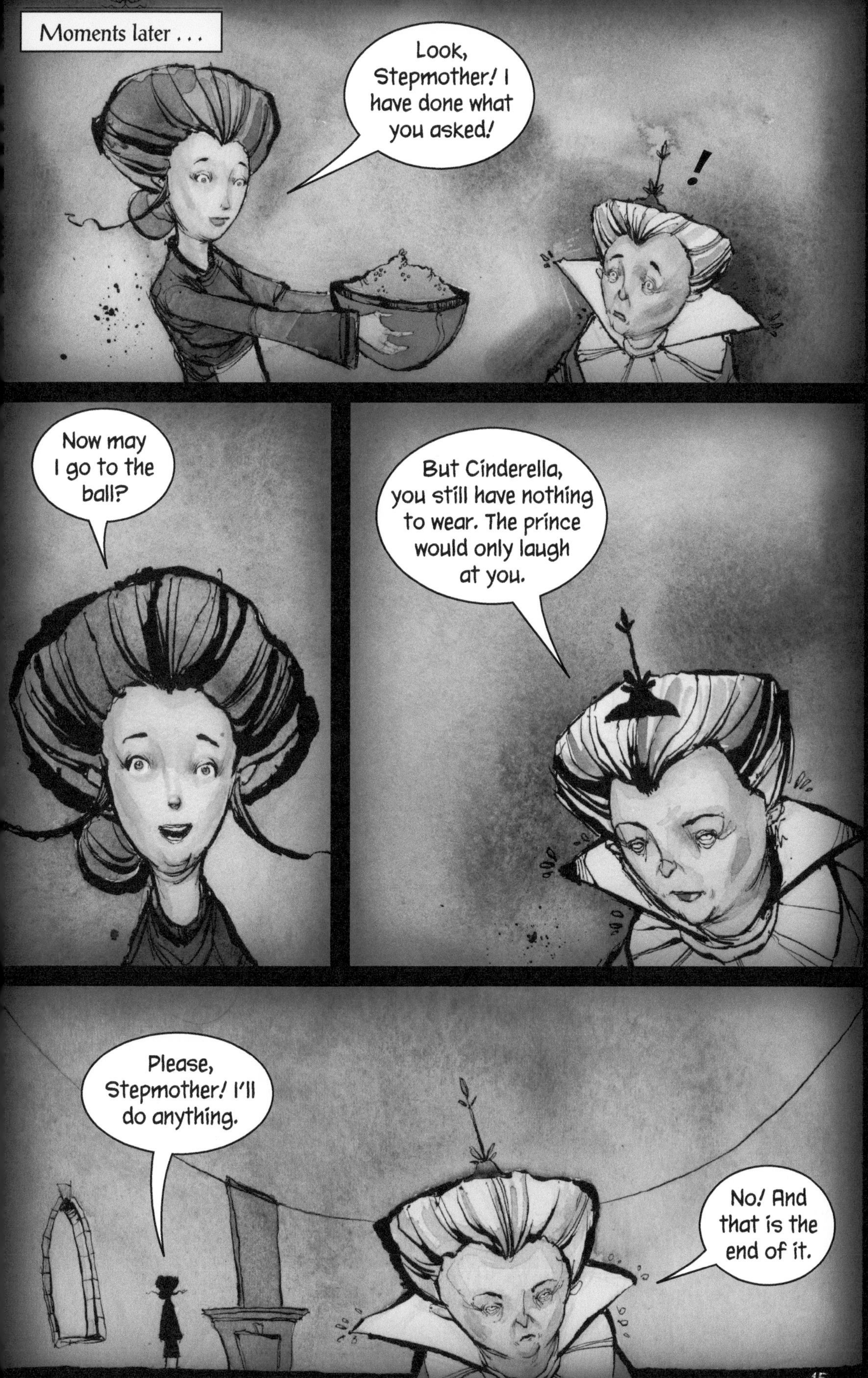

Moments later . . .
Look, Stepmother! I have done what you asked!
!
Now may I go to the ball?
But Cinderella, you still have nothing to wear. The prince would only laugh at you.
Please, Stepmother! I'll do anything.
No! And that is the end of it.

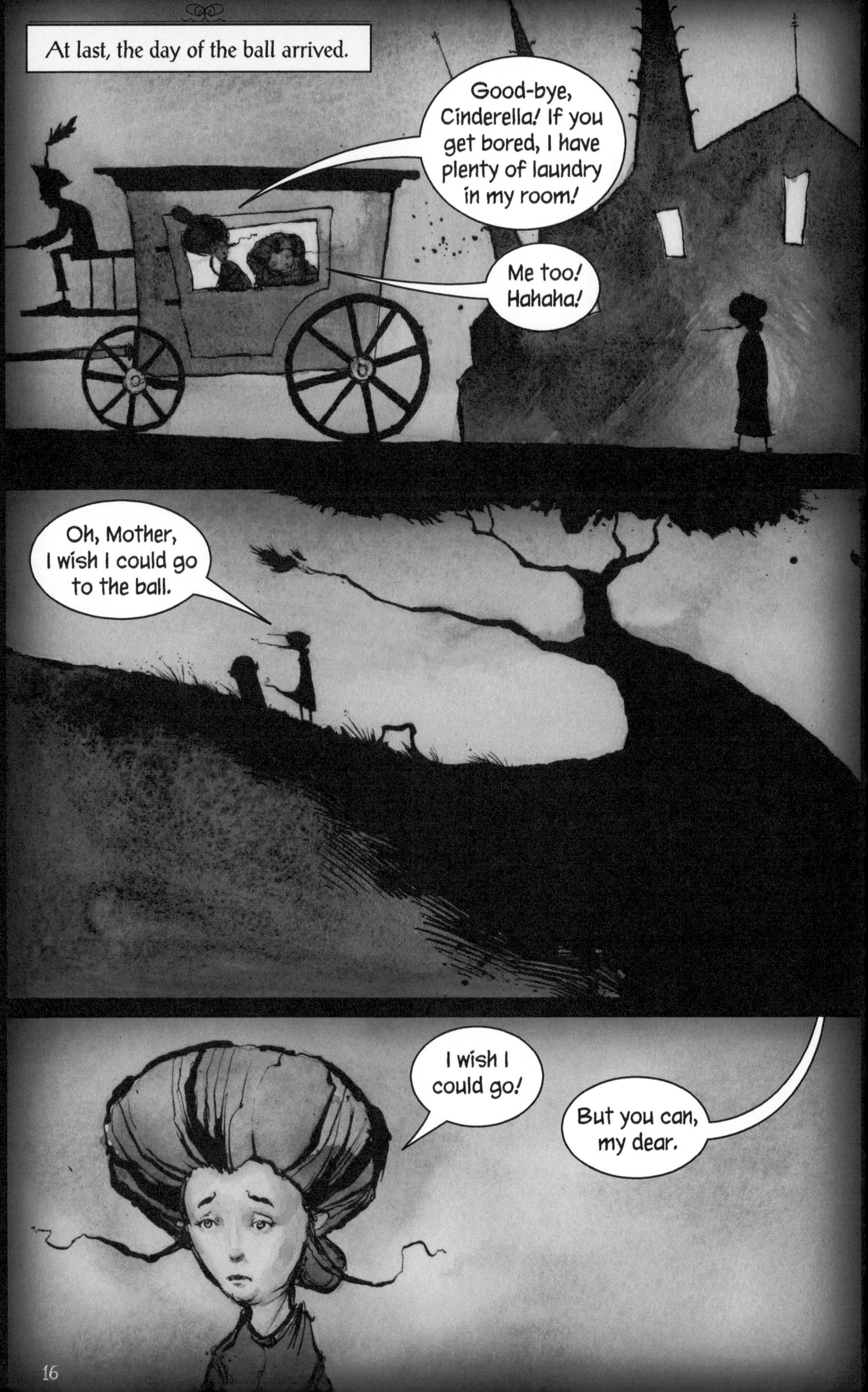
At last, the day of the ball arrived.
Good-bye, Cinderella! If you get bored, I have plenty of laundry in my room!
Me too! Hahaha!
Oh, Mother, I wish I could go to the ball.
I wish I could go!
But you can, my dear.

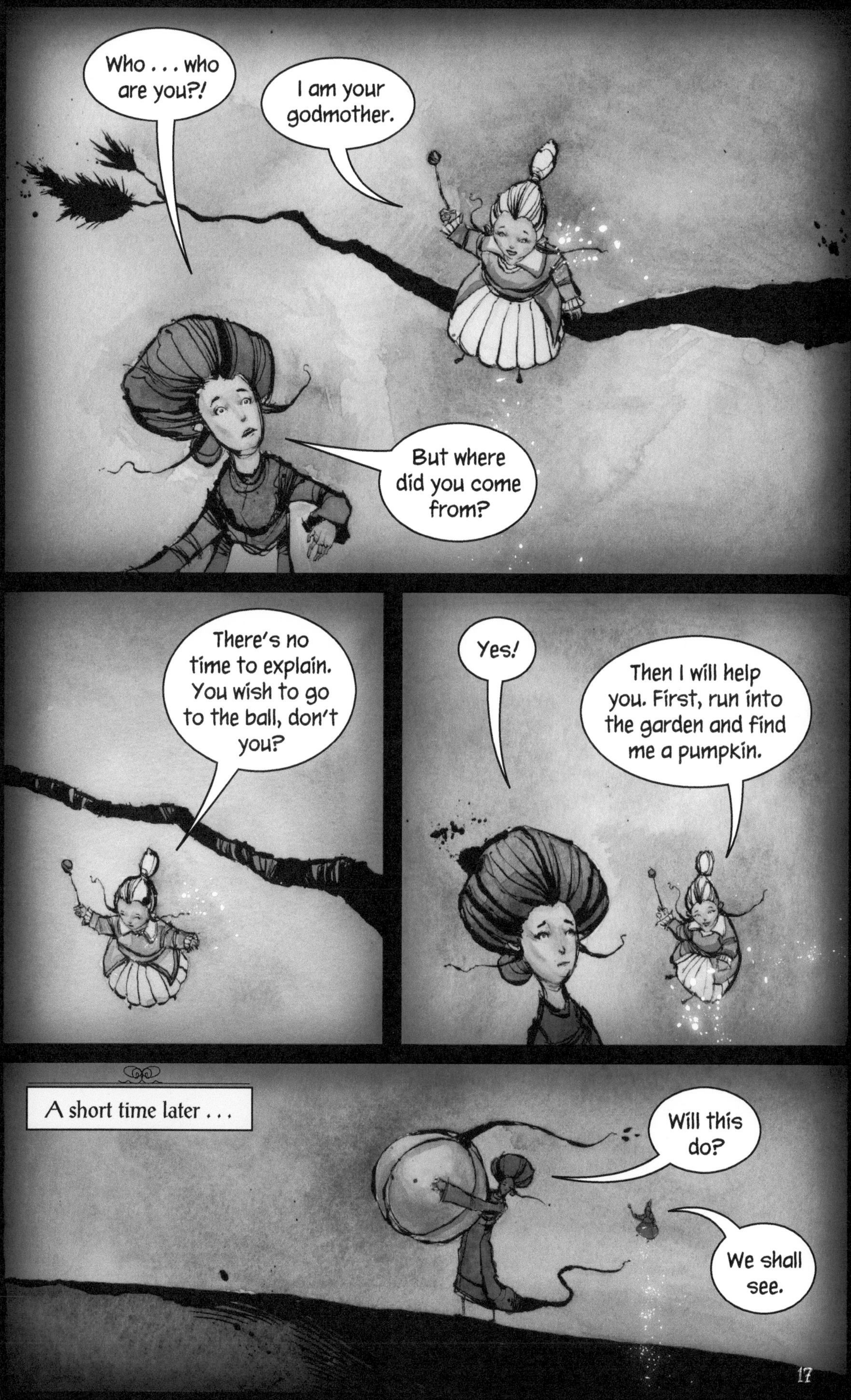
Who . . . who are you?!
I am your godmother.
But where did you come from?
There's no time to explain. You wish to go to the ball, don't you?
Yes!
Then I will help you. First, run into the garden and find me a pumpkin.
A short time later . . .
Will this do?
We shall see.

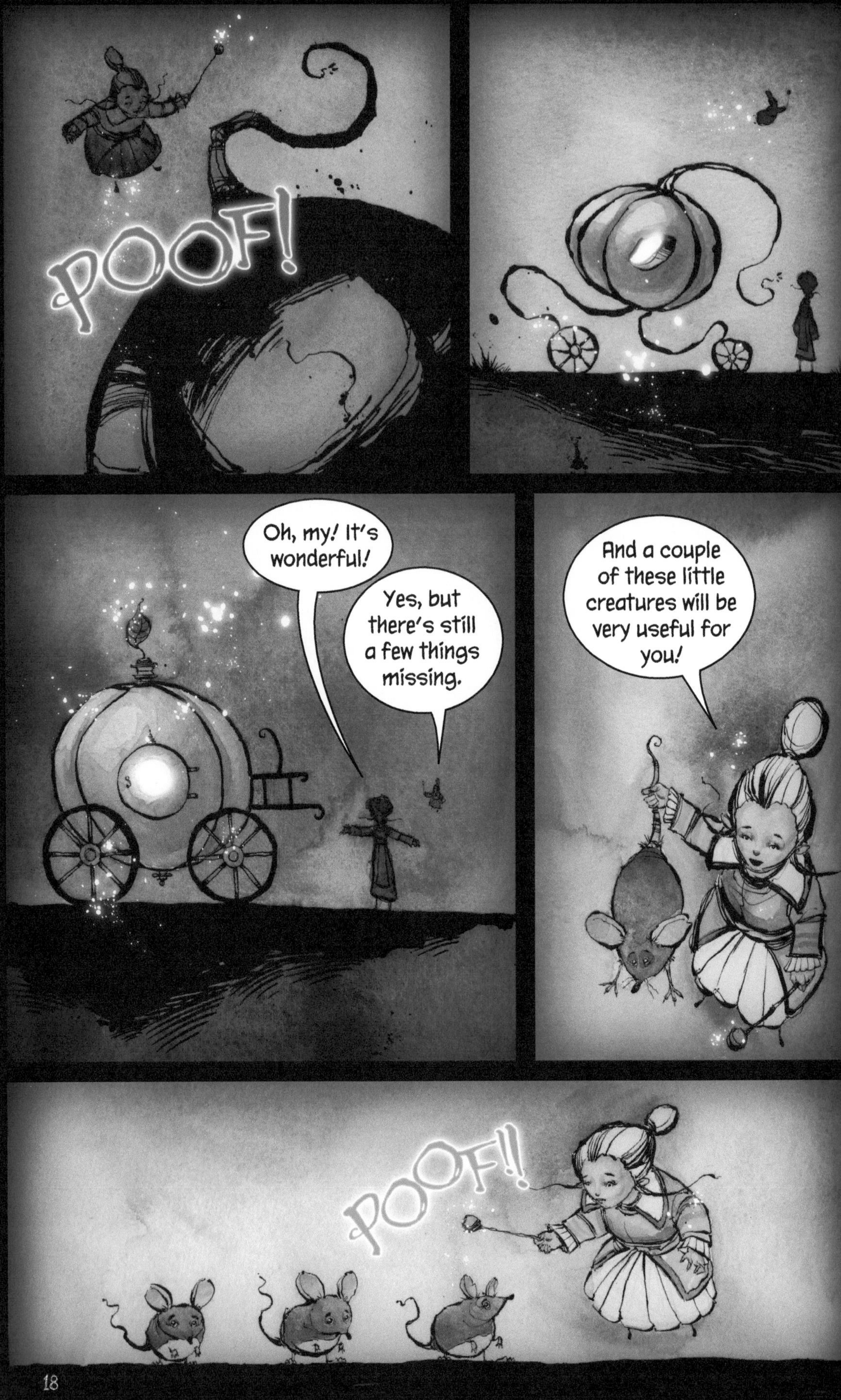
POOF!
Oh, my! It's wonderful!
Yes, but there's still a few things missing.
And a couple of these little creatures will be very useful for you!
POOF!!

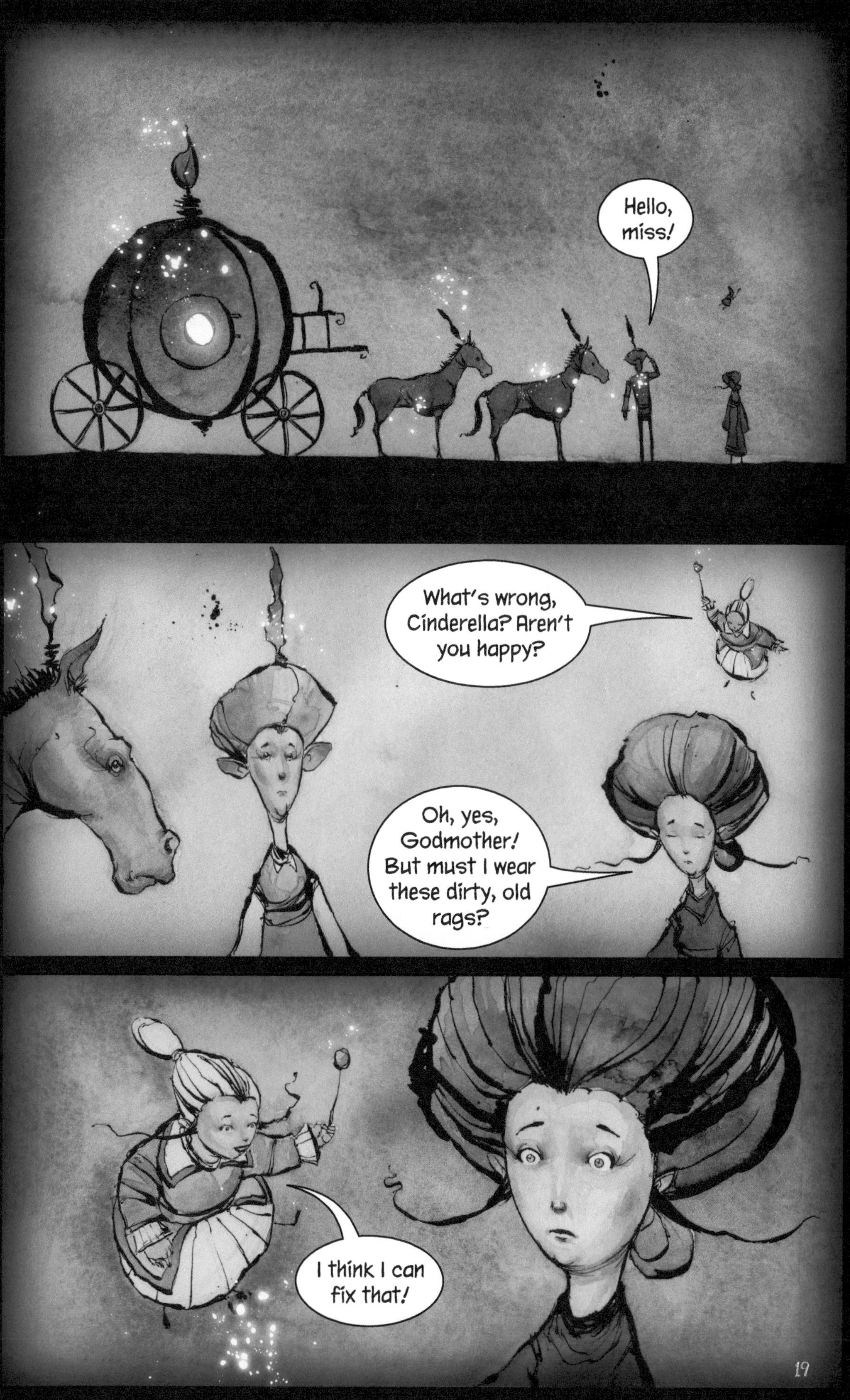
Hello, miss!
What's wrong, Cinderella? Aren't you happy?
Oh, yes, Godmother! But must I wear these dirty, old rags?
I think I can fix that!

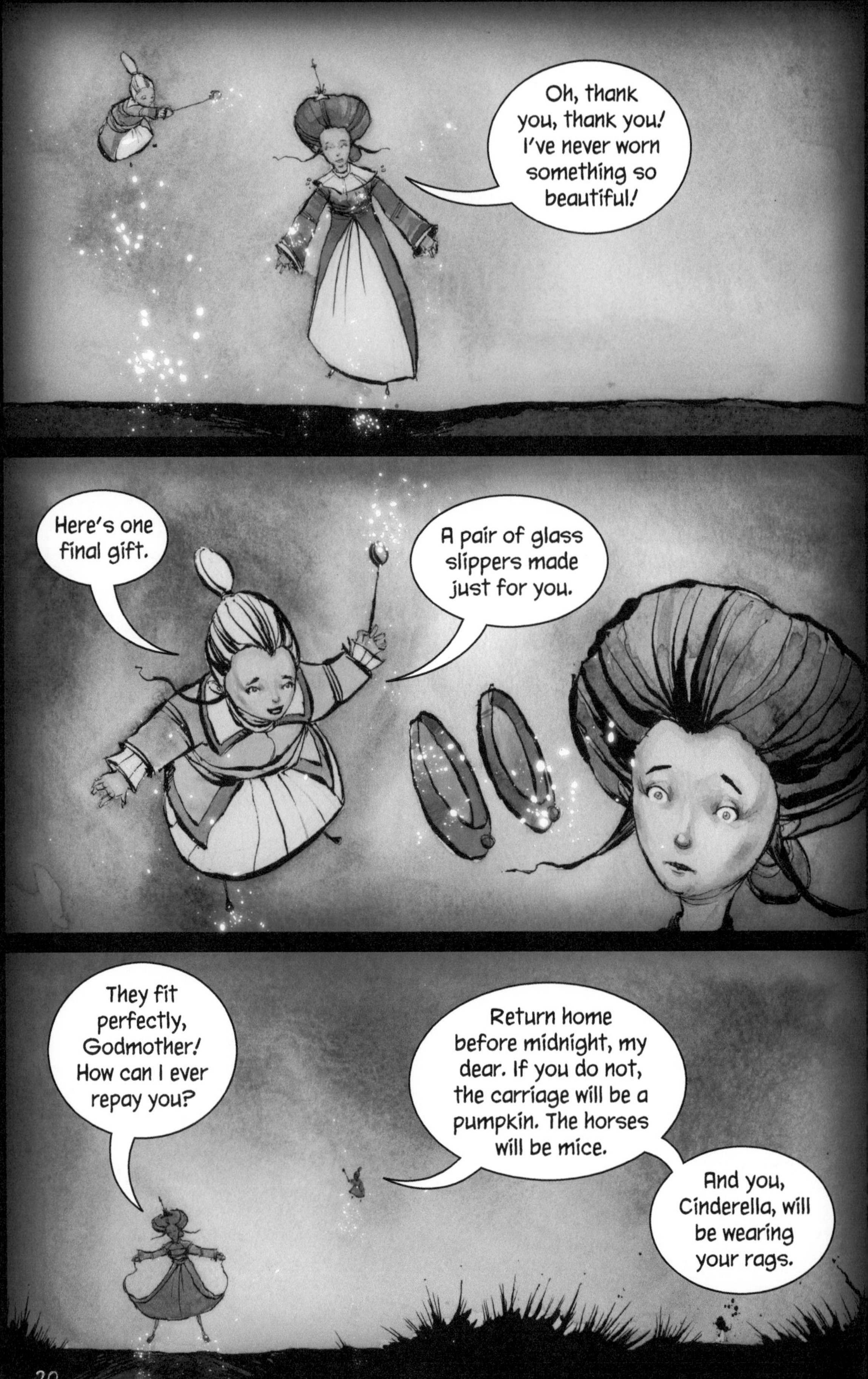
Oh, thank you, thank you! I've never worn something so beautiful!
Here's one final gift.
A pair of glass slippers made just for you.
They fit perfectly, Godmother! How can I ever repay you?
Return home before midnight, my dear. If you do not, the carriage will be a pumpkin. The horses will be mice.
And you, Cinderella, will be wearing your rags.

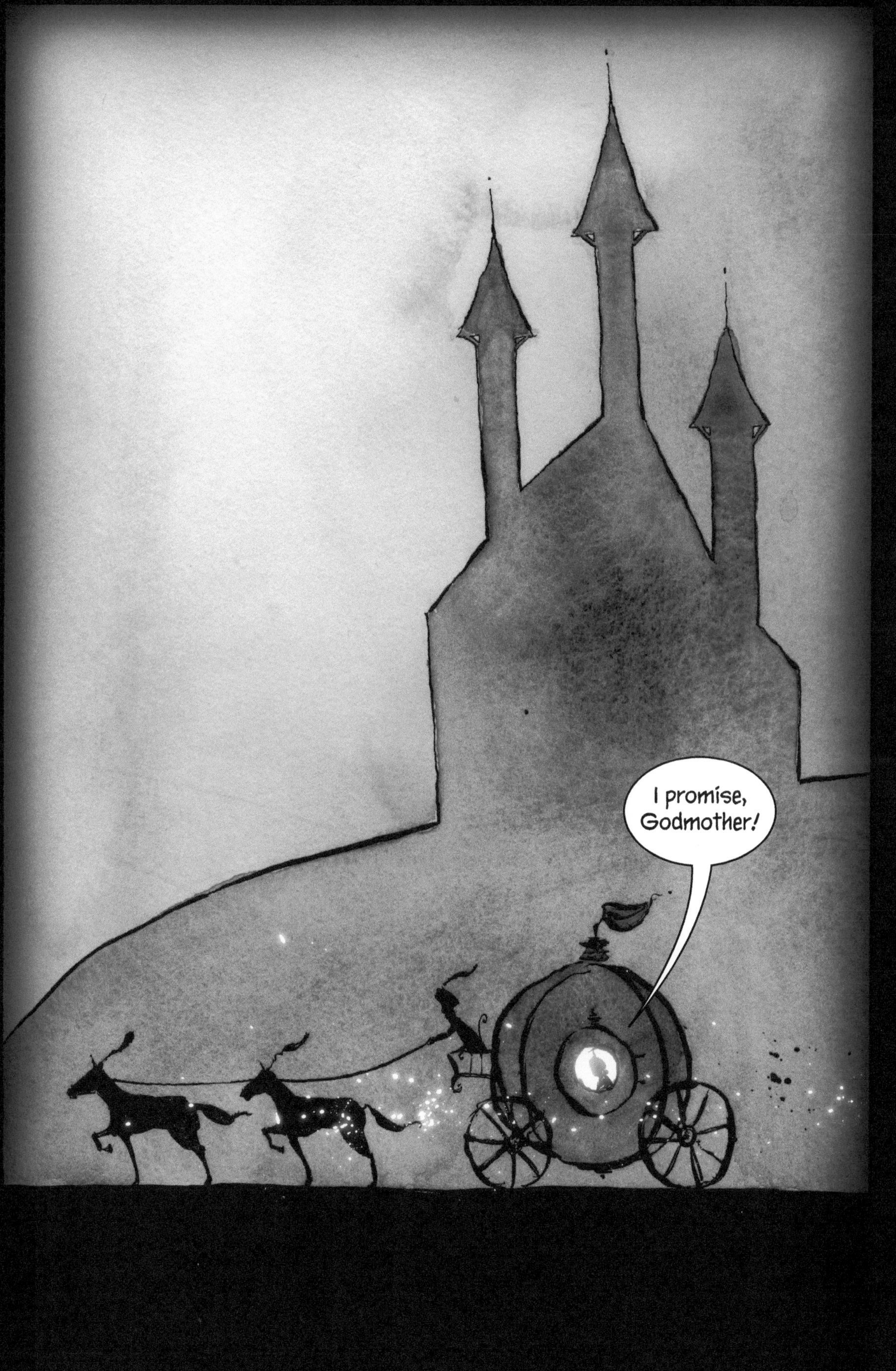
I promise, Godmother!

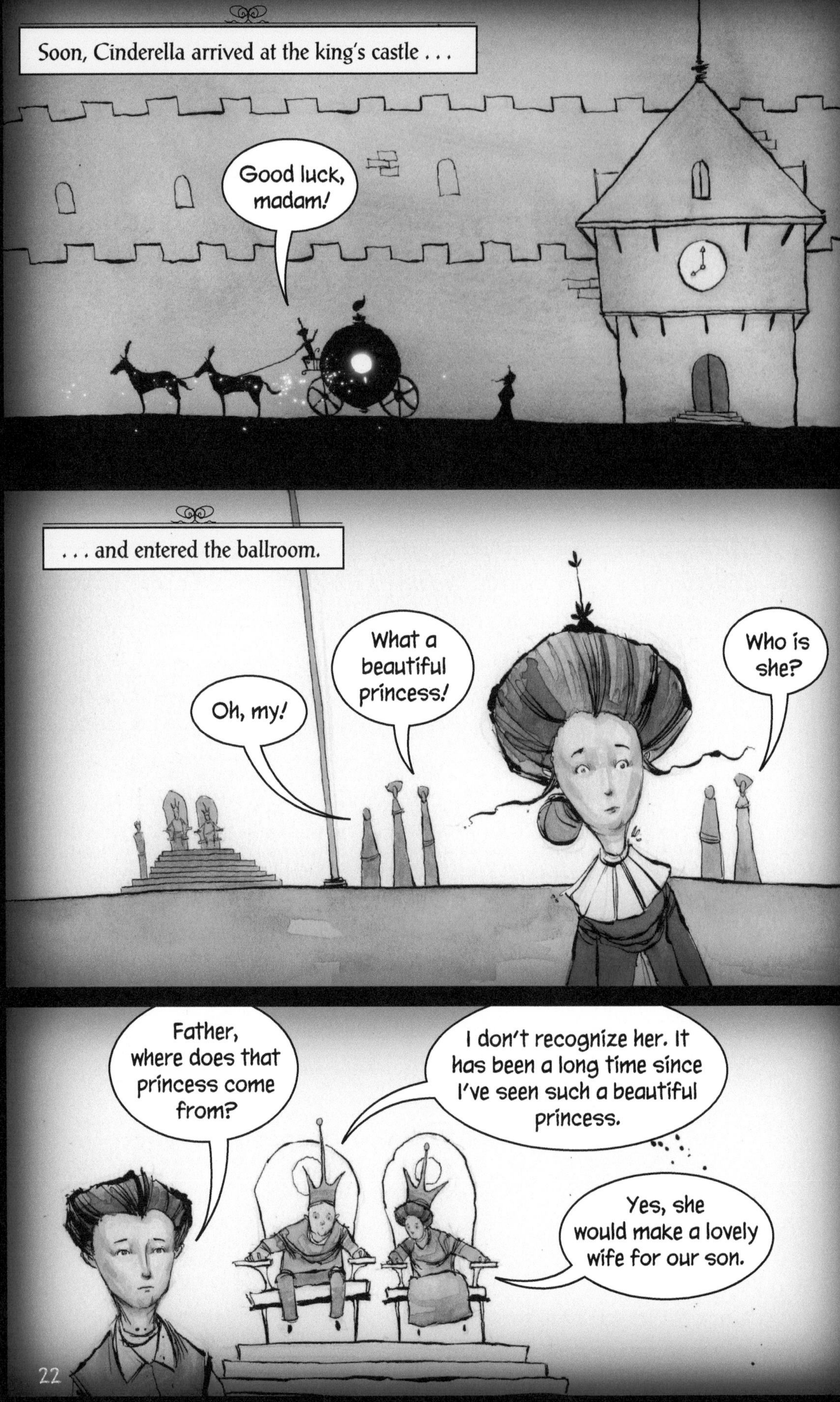
Soon, Cinderella arrived at the king's castle . . .
Good luck, madam!
. . . and entered the ballroom.
Oh, my!
What a beautiful princess!
Who is she?
Father, where does that princess come from?
I don't recognize her. It has been a long time since I've seen such a beautiful princess.
Yes, she would make a lovely wife for our son.

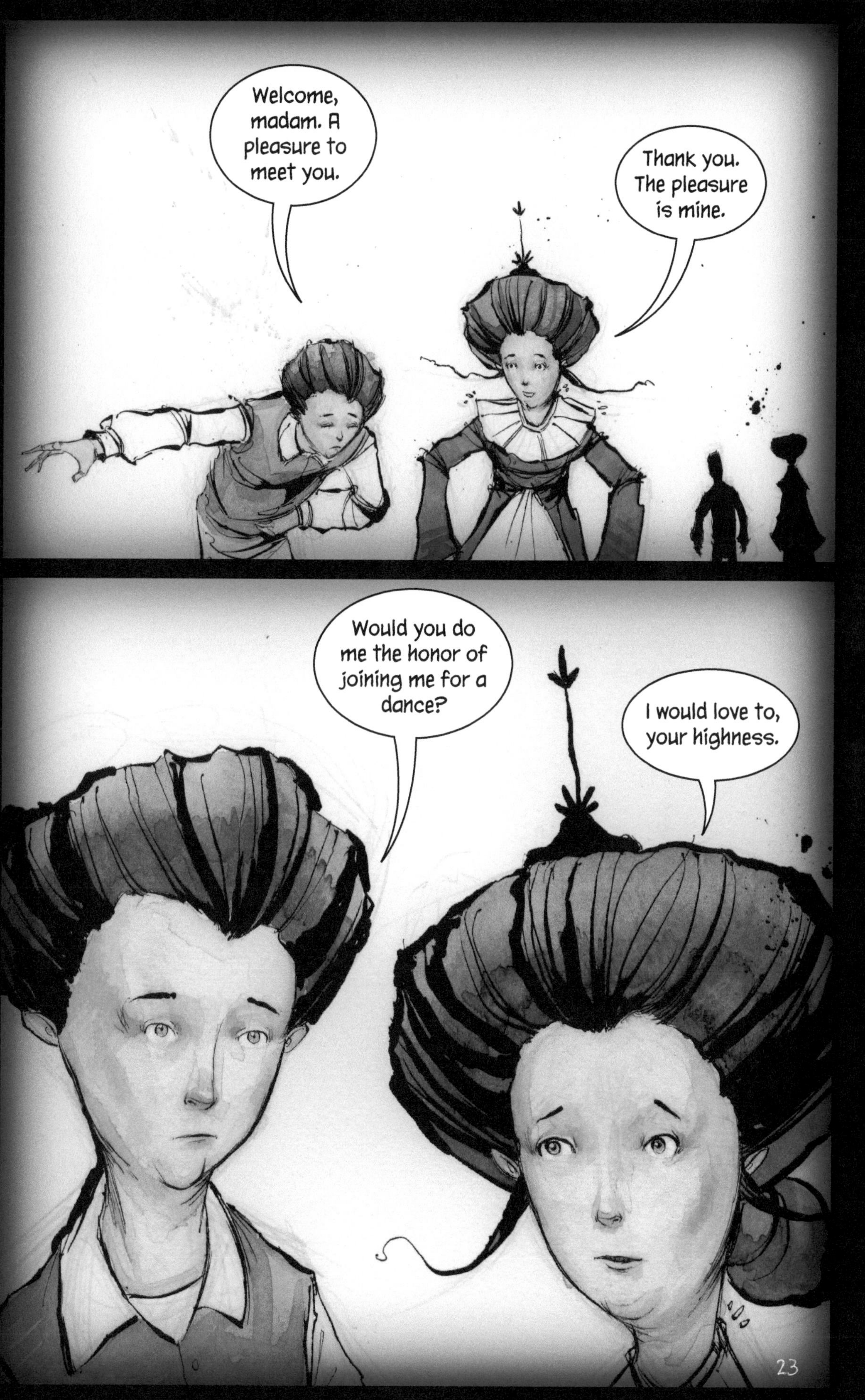
Welcome, madam. A pleasure to meet you.
Thank you. The pleasure is mine.
Would you do me the honor of joining me for a dance?
I would love to, your highness.

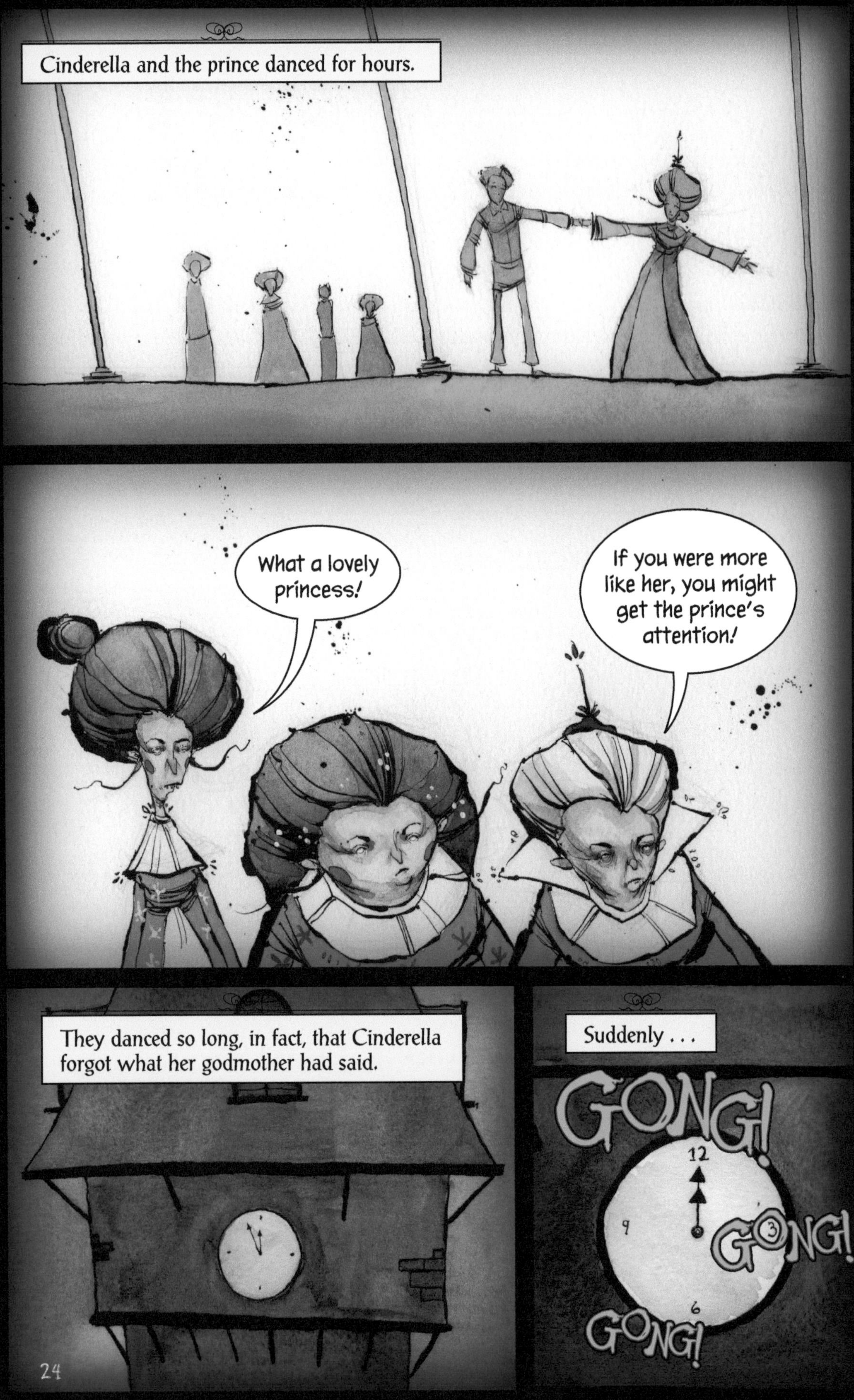
Cinderella and the prince danced for hours.
What a lovely princess!
If you were more like her, you might get the prince's attention!
They danced so long, in fact, that Cinderella forgot what her godmother had said.
Suddenly . . .
GONG!
GONG!
GONG!

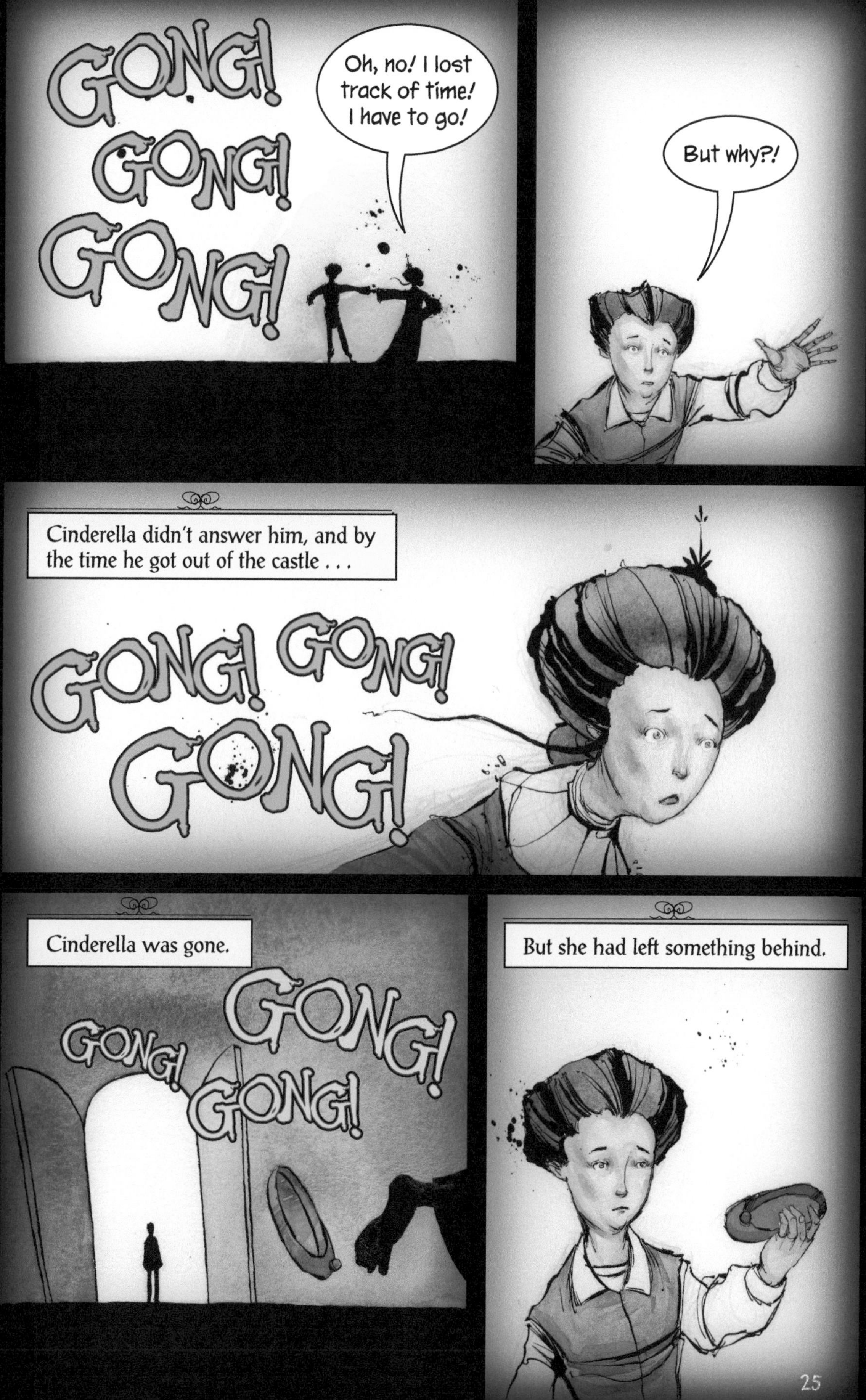
GONG! GONG! GONG!
Oh, no! I lost track of time! I have to go!
But why?!
Cinderella didn't answer him, and by the time he got out of the castle . . .
GONG! GONG! GONG!
Cinderella was gone.
GONG! GONG! GONG!
But she had left something behind.

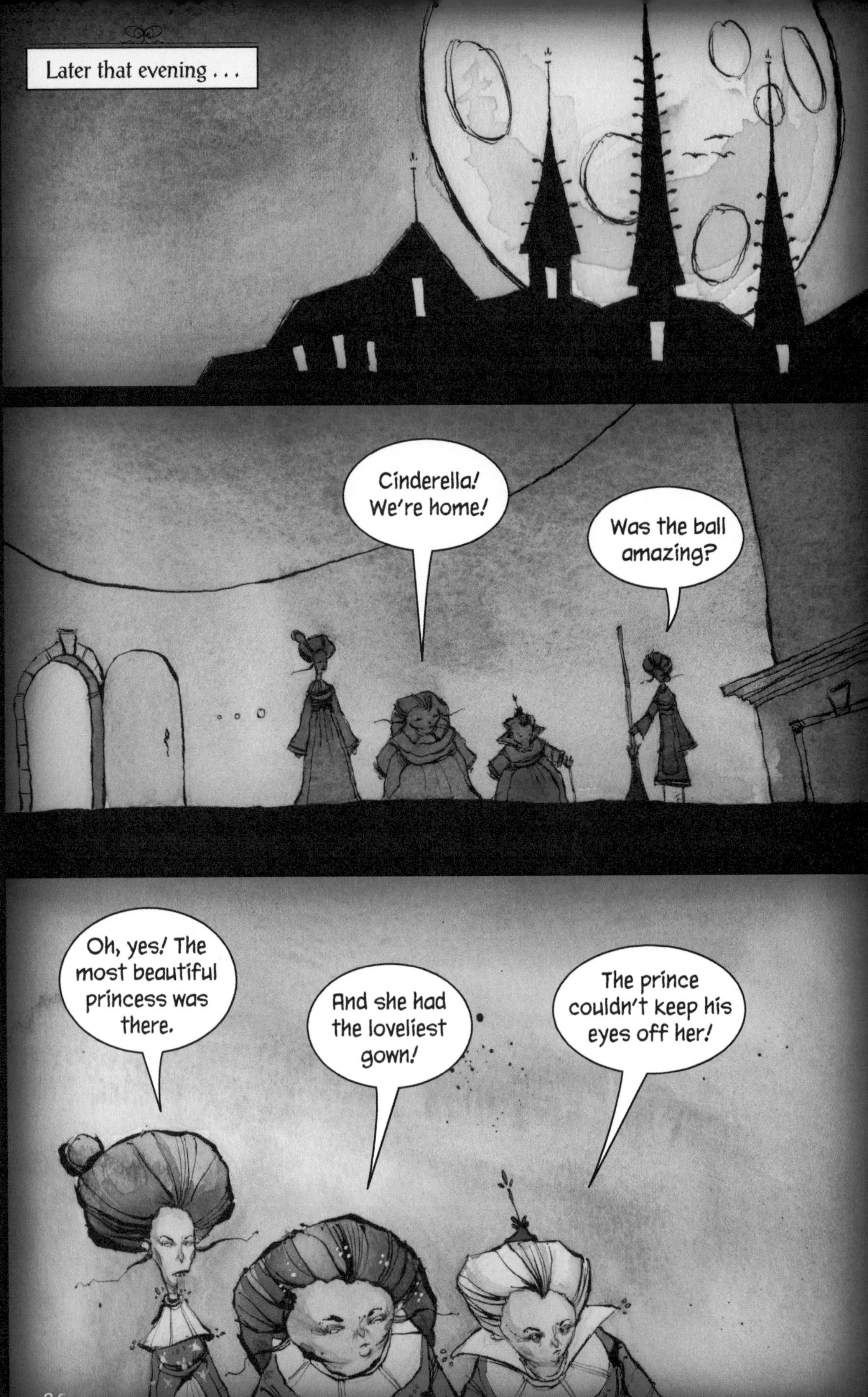
Later that evening . . .
Cinderella! We're home!
Was the ball amazing?
Oh, yes! The most beautiful princess was there.
And she had the loveliest gown!
The prince couldn't keep his eyes off her!

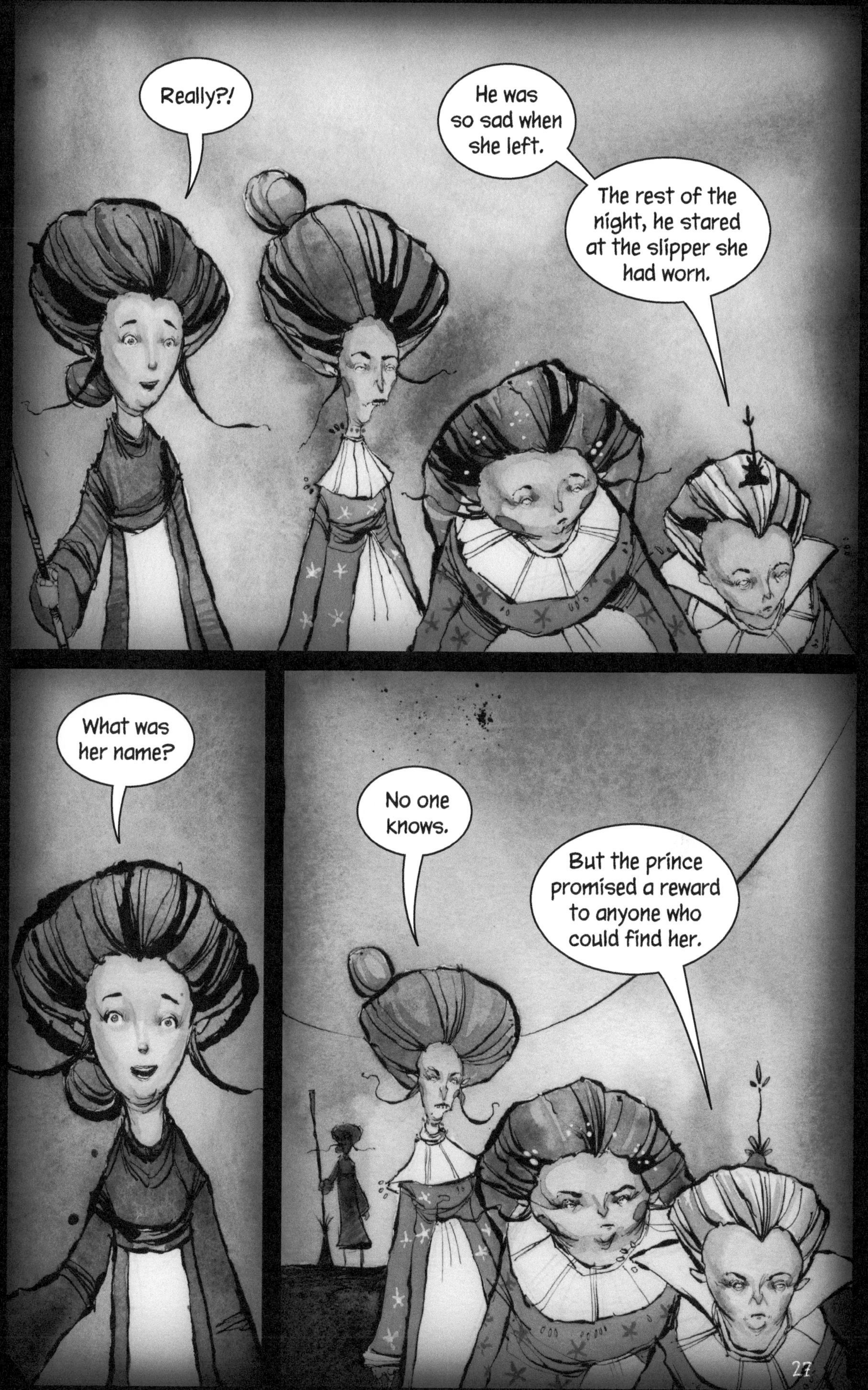
Really?!
He was so sad when she left.
The rest of the night, he stared at the slipper she had worn.
What was her name?
No one knows.
But the prince promised a reward to anyone who could find her.

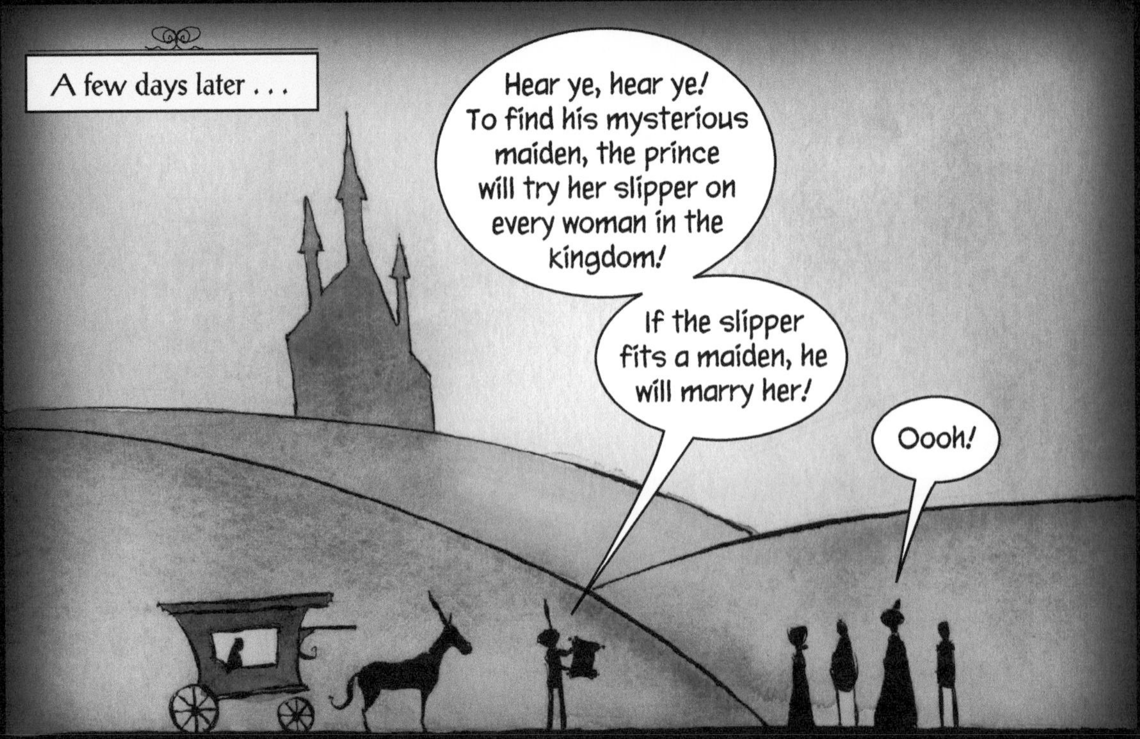
A few days later . . .
Hear ye, hear ye! To find his mysterious maiden, the prince will try her slipper on every woman in the kingdom!
If the slipper fits a maiden, he will marry her!
Oooh!

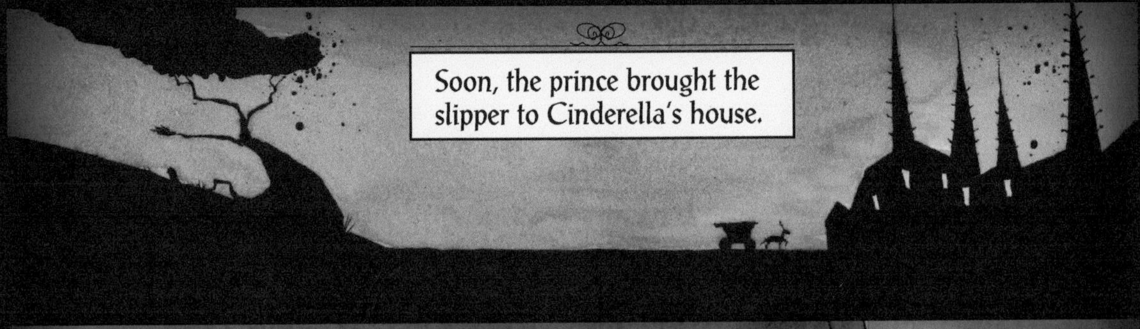
Soon, the prince brought the slipper to Cinderella's house.

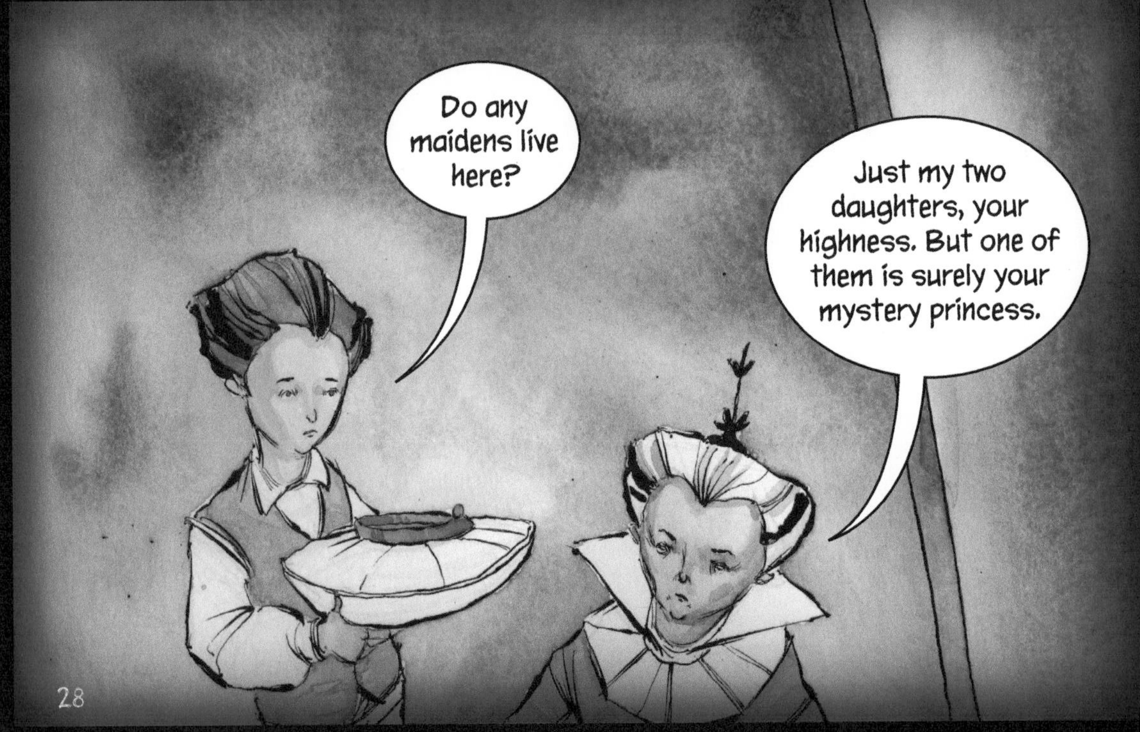
Do any maidens live here?
Just my two daughters, your highness. But one of them is surely your mystery princess.

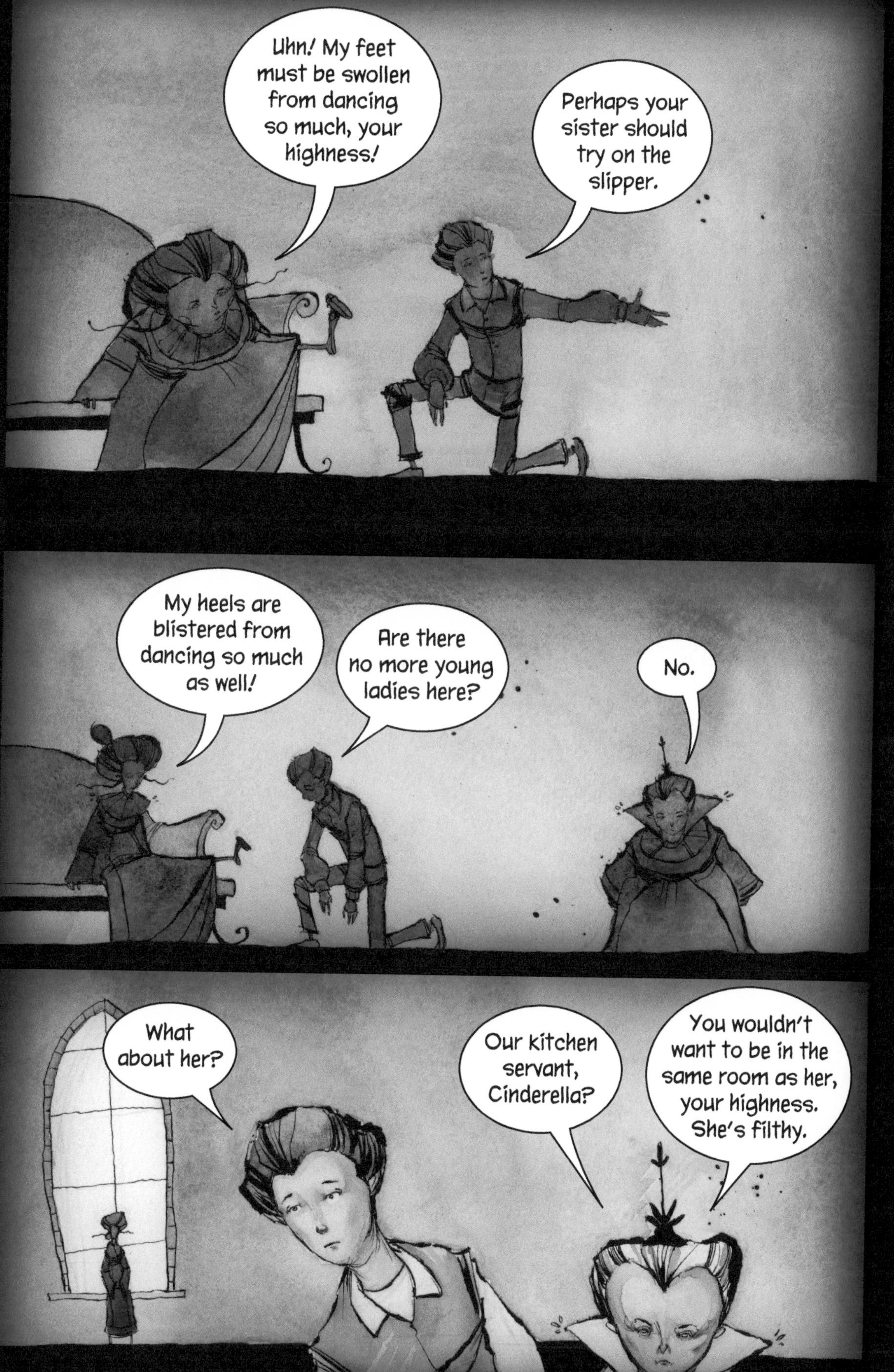
Uhn! My feet must be swollen from dancing so much, your highness!
Perhaps your sister should try on the slipper.
My heels are blistered from dancing so much as well!
Are there no more young ladies here?
No.
What about her?
Our kitchen servant, Cinderella?
You wouldn't want to be in the same room as her, your highness. She's filthy.

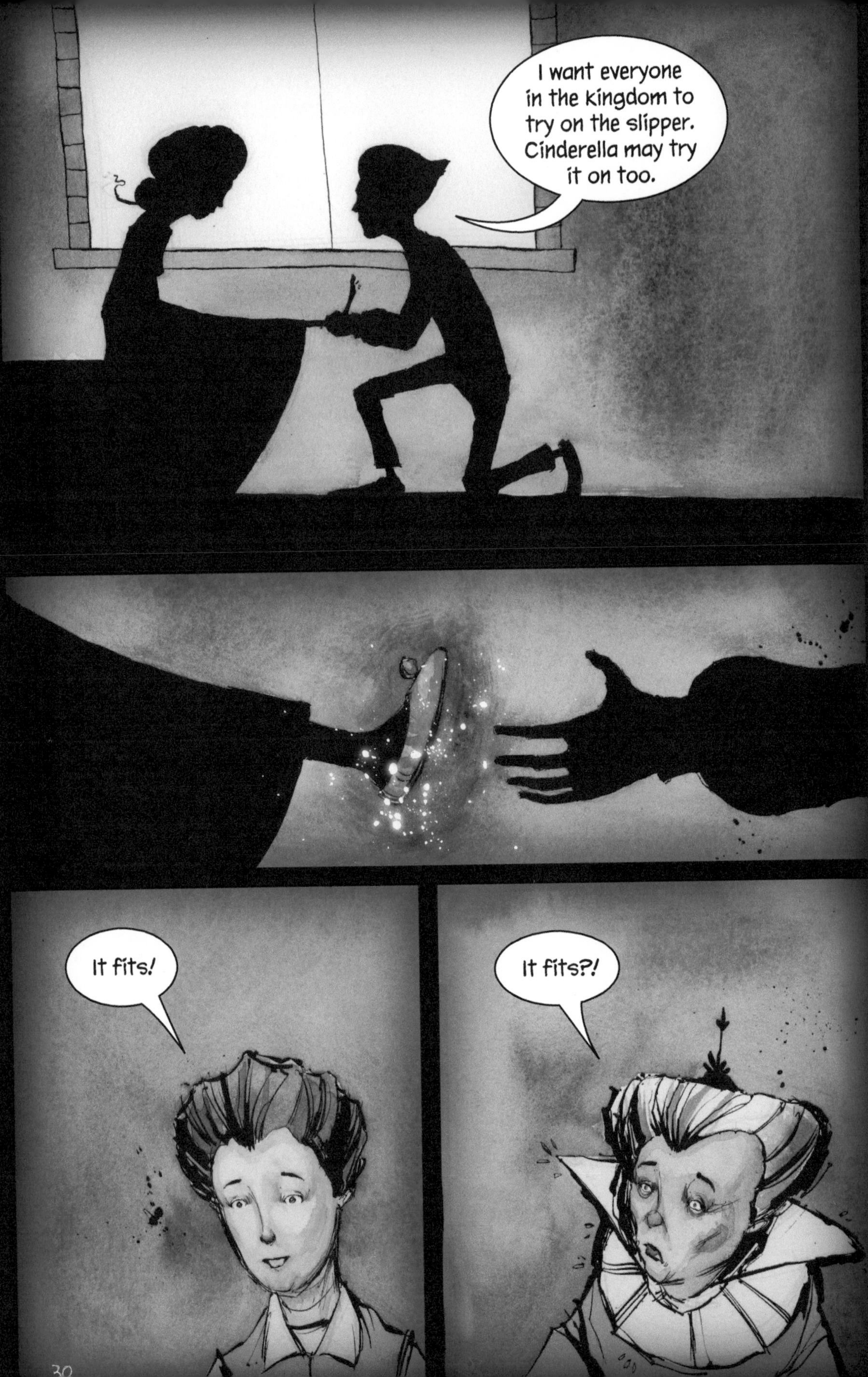
I want everyone in the kingdom to try on the slipper. Cinderella may try it on too.
It fits!
It fits?!

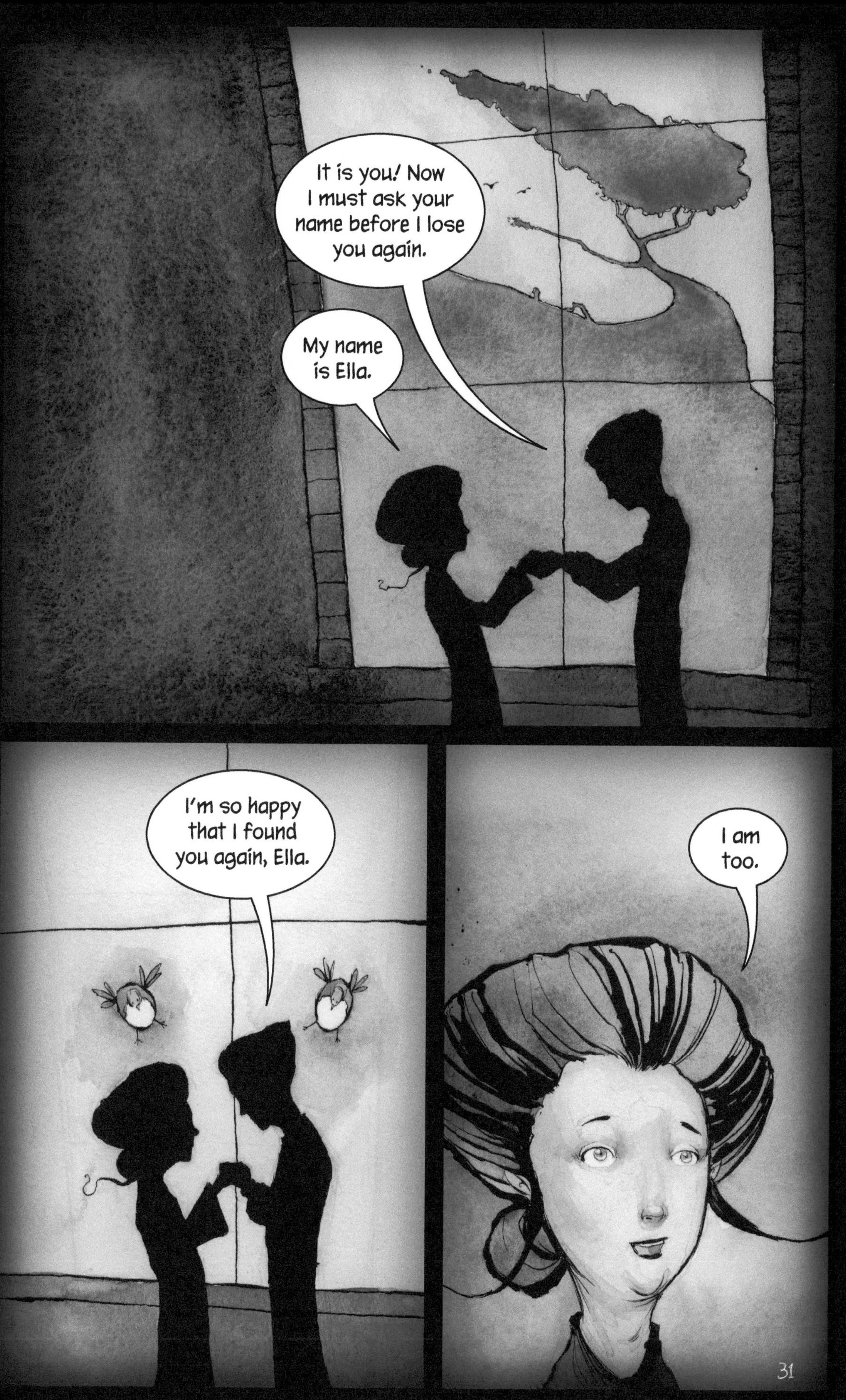
It is you! Now I must ask your name before I lose you again.
My name is Ella.
I'm so happy that I found you again, Ella.
I am too.

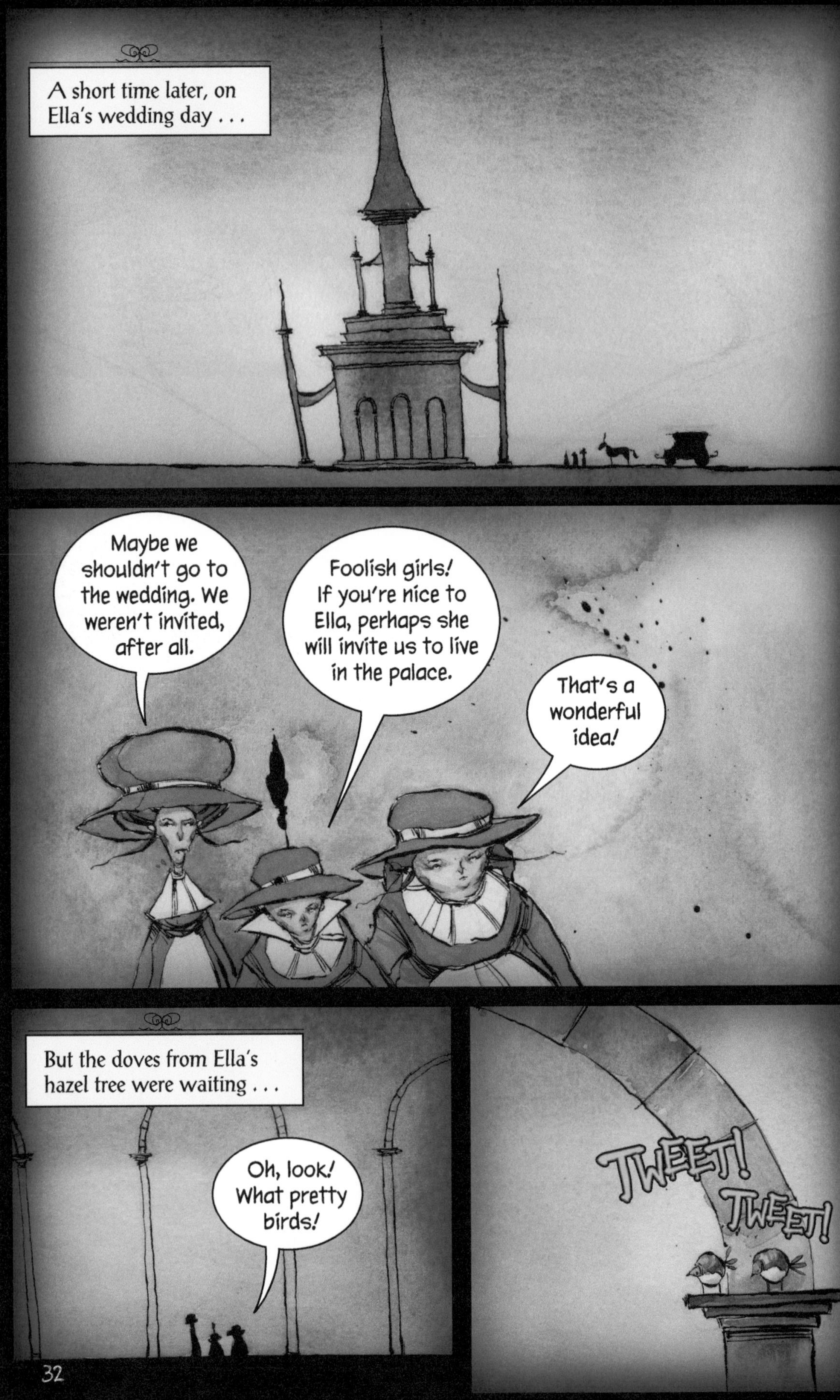
A short time later, on Ella's wedding day . . .
Maybe we shouldn't go to the wedding. We weren't invited, after all.
Foolish girls! If you're nice to Ella, perhaps she will invite us to live in the palace.
That's a wonderful idea!
But the doves from Ella's hazel tree were waiting . . .
Oh, look! What pretty birds!
TWEET! TWEET!

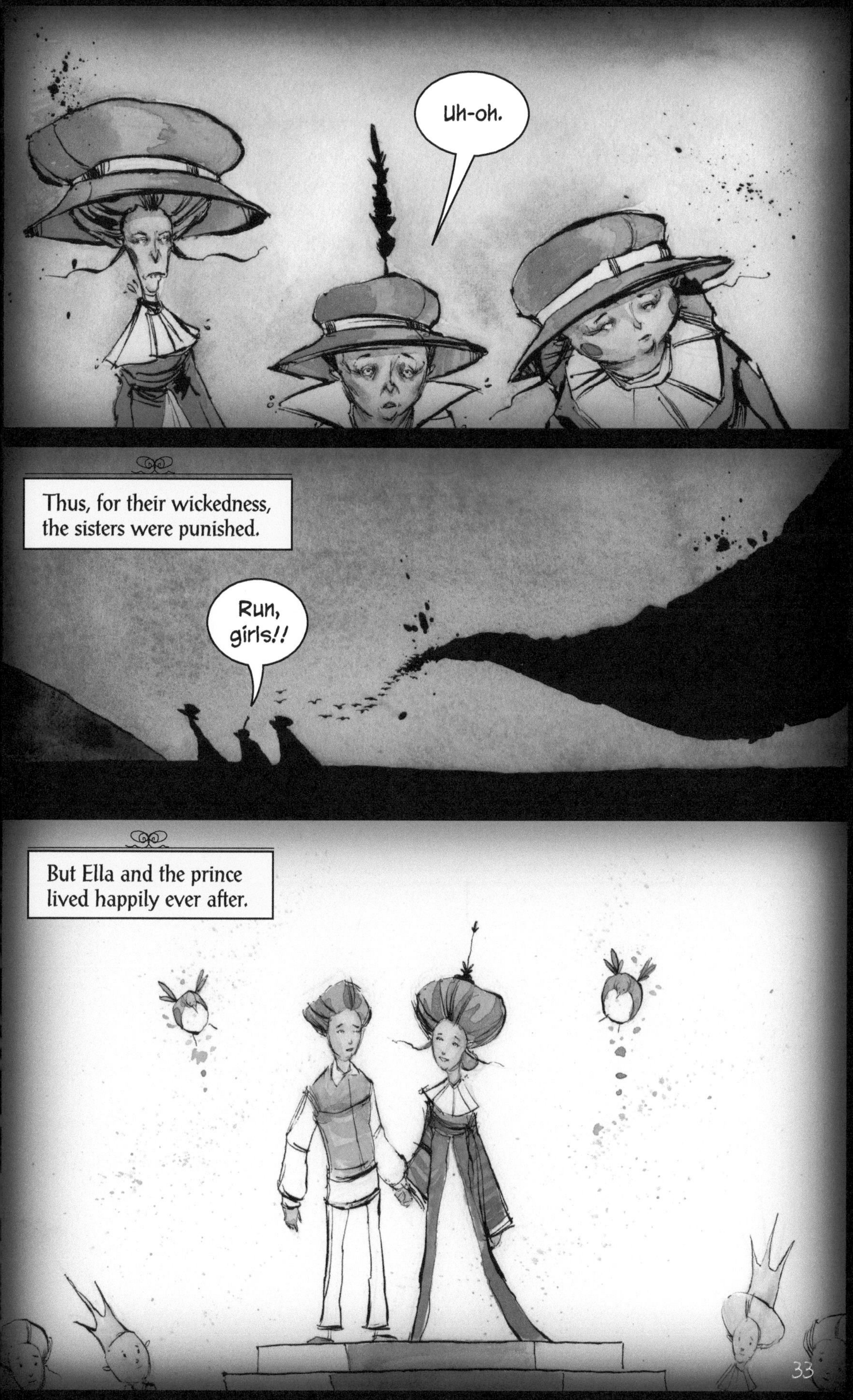
Uh-oh.
Thus, for their wickedness, the sisters were punished.
Run, girls!!
But Ella and the prince lived happily ever after.

ABOUT THE AUTHOR

Beth Bracken is a children's book editor. She lives in St. Paul, Minnesota, with her husband, Steve, and their dog, Harry, a Jack Russell terrier who thinks he's a lion. When she's not reading, writing, or editing books, Beth spends most of her time knitting endlessly while watching reruns of old TV shows and drinking lots of tea.

ABOUT THE ILLUSTRATOR

Jeffrey Stewart Timmins was born July 2, 1979. In 2003, he graduated from the Classical Animation program at Sheridan College in Oakville, Ontario. He currently works as a freelance designer and animator. Even as an adult, Timmins still holds onto a few important items from his childhood, such as his rubber boots, cape, and lenseless sunglasses.

GLOSSARY

ashamed (uh-SHAMED)—felt embarrassed and guilty

ball (BAWL)—a formal party where people dance and interact

cinders (SIN-durz)—small pieces of wood or coal that have been partly burned

disgusting (diss-GUST-ting)—very unpleasant to others

godmother (GOD-muhth-ur)—a woman who protects a child beginning at birth

hearth (HARTH)—the area in front of a fireplace

highness (HYE-ness)—a title given to members of a royal family

madam (MAD-uhm)—a formal title for a woman

messenger (MESS-uhn-jur)—someone who delivers messages

miserable (MIZ-ur-uh-buhl)—sad or unhappy

proclamation (prok-luh-MAY-shuhn)—a public announcement

turtledoves (TUR-tuhl-duhvz)—small, wild, friendly birds

vile (VILE)—evil or immoral

THE HISTORY OF CINDERELLA

The story of Cinderella has been told for hundreds of years in more than a thousand different ways. In fact, the earliest known version dates back to about A.D. 860. That's more than 1,100 years old! It appeared in a Chinese book of legends called *Miscellaneous Morsel from Youyang.* The author, Tuan Ch'eng-Shih, titled the story "Ye Xian." Although the title was different, many parts were the same as today's versions of Cinderella, including the evil stepmother and a pair of golden slippers.

For many years after, people told the tale of Cinderella. They passed the story orally from person to person, meaning it was never written down. In 1634, Italian Giambattista Basile finally recorded the tale again for his book *The Tale of Tales, or Entertainment for Little Ones.* Many believe Basile's book inspired some of the most popular versions of Cinderella.

In 1697, Frenchman Charles Perrault based his version off of Basile's work. However, Perrault also added his own twist on the tale. He introduced a fairy godmother, and he added a pumpkin carriage and a few animal servants. He also made the famous slippers glass instead of gold.

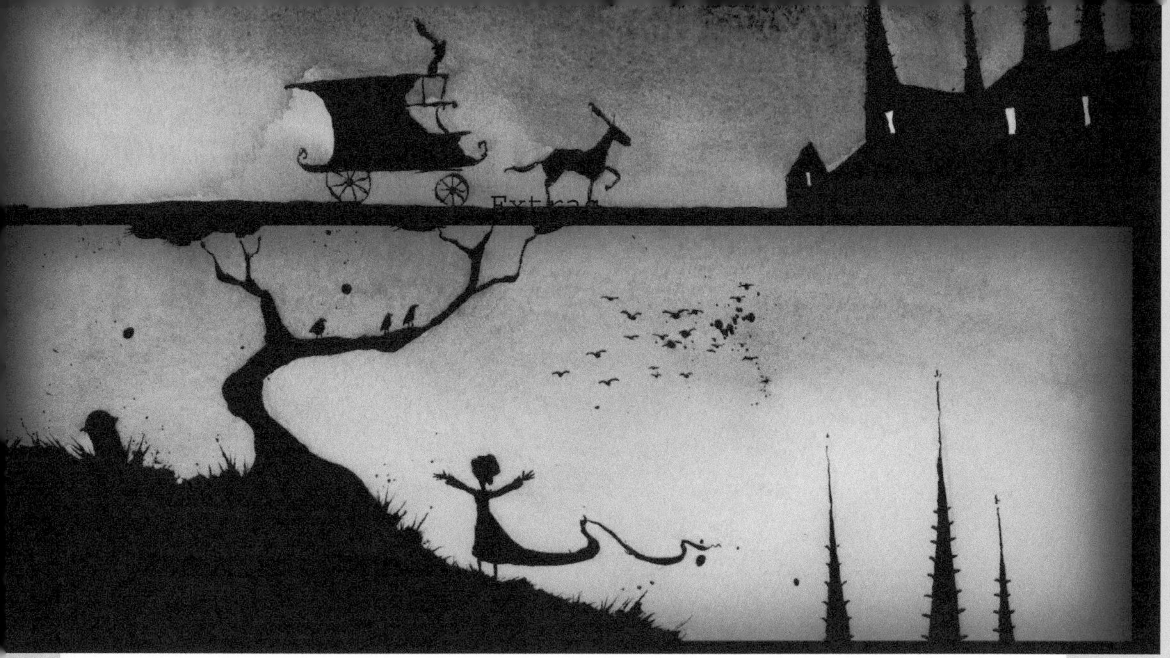

In the early 1800s, brothers Jacob and Wilhelm Grimm, two famous fairy tale writers, created yet another version. They called the story "Aschenputtel," or "Ash Girl." In their tale, the stepsisters are punished for being mean to Cinderella. At the end, the sisters' eyes are pecked out by doves!

Of the many versions, however, Disney's Cinderella remains one of the most famous. Released in theaters on February 15, 1950, Cinderella quickly became one of the highest-grossing films of the year. It has inspired even more versions of this famous tale.

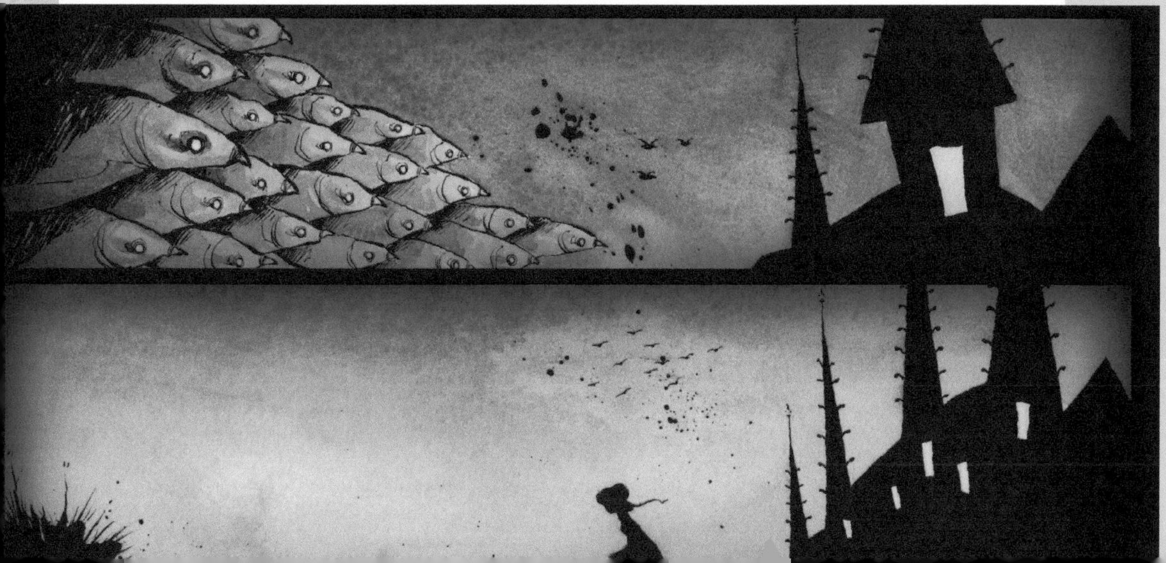

DISCUSSION QUESTIONS

1. Why didn't the prince care that Cinderella was dusty and dirty? What does his reaction tell you about his character?

2. Each page of a graphic novel has several illustrations called panels. What is your favorite panel in this book? Describe what you like about the illustration and why it's your favorite.

3. Fairy tales are often told over and over again. Have you heard the Cinderella fairy tale before? How is this version of the story different from other versions you've heard, seen, or read?

WRITING PROMPTS

1. Fairy tales are fantasy stories, often about wizards, goblins, giants, and fairies. Many fairy tales have a happy ending. Write your own fairy tale. Then, read it to a friend or family member.

2. Pretend you have a fairy godmother that could grant you three wishes. What three things would you ask for and why?

3. Write your own version of Cinderella using people you know as the characters. Who will be the fairy godmother? Who will be the evil stepsisters? You can even make yourself a character!

INTERNET SITES

The book may be over, but the adventure is just beginning.

Do you want to read more about the subjects or ideas in this book? Want to play cool games or watch videos about the authors who write these books? Then go to FactHound. At *www.facthound.com*, you'll be able to do all that, and more. The FactHound website can also send you to other safe Internet sites.

CHECK IT OUT